CW00516360

Night Duty, West End

Night Duty, West End

Published by The Conrad Press in the United Kingdom 2021

Tel: +44(0)1227 472 874
www.theconradpress.com
info@theconradpress.com

ISBN 978-1-913567-96-5

Copyright © David O'Kane, 2021

The moral right of David O'Kane to be identified as author of this work has been asserted in accordance with the Copyright, Designs and Patents Act 1988.

All rights reserved.

Disclaimer:
No one character is based on any one individual, though composite characters have been formed. Events are based on myth and composite incidents and may factually bare some resemblance to events in the past.

Typesetting and Cover Design by: Charlotte Mouncey, www.bookstyle.co.uk

The Conrad Press logo was designed by Maria Priestley.

Printed and bound in Great Britain by Clays Ltd, Elcograf S.p.A.

Night Duty, West End

David O'Kane

Prologue

Kath Peters was due for promotion in the next few weeks, and she had taken a few minutes to look back over the pictures and the collection of paper she had in her desk as she cleared everything out. As she moved through the drawers, she had uncovered a few more memories and this in turn had prompted her to allow herself the luxury to drift for a few moments and recollect her probation. She reflected on how much the job had changed over the years since then and the changes that she still felt were needed to move the Met into the 21st Century.

Squashed in the bottom drawer was her soft white hat from her probation. They wore hard bowlers now, health and safety, well at least that was better a move forward. The golden 'Dixon of Dock Green' age, was it real? Did the 1980s hold the key to the policing of the future? As far back as she could remember the 1980s was a different time and it was a time when the policing reflected the population's needs. She delved deeper into her memories and she still came up with the question; did the police reflect what the people deserved? If that was the case what did the people deserve now?

The day-to-day policing had remained the same. The police officers she had entered the police service with, that is service now, not force, as it was in her day, were older and wiser most if not all retired or retiring. They were still the police officers from the past. They were still the ones who had been accountable for policing actions that in today's policing would see investigations yet in those times were what the police did and how they did it. It was also what was expected from the public too, the get the job done regardless of the consequences worked then but looking back it created many more problems when examined with today's lens. In fact, she mused, the investigations of the present were very much about the solution, the policing solutions, of the past. Were they appropriate and were they a reflection of the needs of the times?

Policing the 1980s had been about miners and strikes as well as about the day-to-day policing of the West End of London. It was about the bombs and the hoaxes and well as the shoplifters and the drug dealers. Somewhere in there in her initial posting area was the prostitutes and the peep show too. Nowadays policing was similar, it was about the latest terrorist ordeal or threat, and the impact parochially and internationally of incidents across this capital.

She reshaped her white hat and put it onto her head, turning towards the mirror on the wall and looked at how old she had become. On her shoulders was a variety of rank generated insignia that showed she has progressed up the ranks. But the face that stared back at her was still the one that had started her policing career way back when she was a youngster. Soon she would be Commissioner. She would never have even considered this all those years ago. Now it was a conclusion she had striven for over the last few years, aspiring always to improve on what she had done before. Her mind came back from the past as she sipped her tea. She had a few more hours before the car came to collect her for the dinner. She sipped her tea again and allowed herself the luxury of remembering those first days as a police officer.

Chapter One

Night duty

It was cold, very cold. The wind seemed to find its way into every gap of the uniform and bite into the skin beneath. The winter night's discomfort was made worse as the probationer felt she could not call for the GP car, the 'General Purpose' car, to pick her up and take her around her beat. She felt she would be ridiculed by the old sweats because she was weak, a woman and a probationer. She had heard what they called WPCs, 'slit arses', and it made her skin crawl with contempt that these people were so brutal with their language. She could not hide away as she was bound to get caught. The skipper had said as much; 'I will be watching you, just give me an excuse, I don't like plonks and I don't like probationers, so a plonk probationer, God help the relief'.

She turned the corner, and she was in a small alley away from the hustle and bustle of the night-time Mayfair traffic. She had heard that the posher 'Toms', prostitutes, took their clients here. She again remembered the street duties skipper telling her last week that the Toms were out of bounds for probationers. She had only weeks in the job and she would not be allowed to arrest them until she had her 'Street Duties 2' course. She would have to have eighteen months in before she was taught about the finer points of Toms. The old sweat PC on her street duties had said, 'plonks, property and prostitutes were the downfall of PCs' she was not in a rush then to get to grips with the Toms.

Curiosity had her peering into the corners in the alley-way. She had a sheltered upbringing, well it seemed so, and compared to other people she had met at Hendon training school. She found she was curious about how women could take 'clients', she laughed to herself, no pun intended, in the alleyways. How could men pay for sex? In an alley? So, she looked, half hoping to see, half worried that she might find someone. She would then have to nick them, and to be truthful she had no idea whatsoever as to what to do.

Even this excitement could not make her feel warm, she shivered and walked faster. The alley was deserted, the streets were deserted, and she was freezing. There was nothing to do. The bank around the corner was lit up again. She could see the cleaner making his way around the ground floor. It would take him at least an hour more to get to the first floor, she had found that out two nights ago. So that would be a good place to go to after her 'refs', her refreshment break, when it was really dead, to get a tea and a warm-up. Could it get any deader? At least three more hours, what could she do now?

Park lane was bustling with cars going North and South. There was an expectation that she got at least one body, an arrest, per shift, or three processes. Processes were summons; 'No seat belts', 'defective lights' or better still, more complex summons would get her brownie points with the section skipper. She flushed again with embarrassment, 'plonks and probationers!' It was not what she expected when she signed up for the police.

Kath Peters, aged just eighteen and a half, had joined the Metropolitan Police at seventeen. She had been a police cadet for nearly a year before being attested to Hendon as a WPC. The studying had been hard for her. She was not particularly academic and learning it all, 'star' reports or 'A' reports, was extremely hard for her. Star reports were word perfect, rote learning reserved for the most important legislation. 'A' reports were learnt just the same but they did not have to be exactly word perfect, though to be frank most were learnt that way anyway.

The cadets had prepared her for this style of learning. Star reports and 'A' reports were old hat to her now. The first she was asked to learn was, 'The primary object of an efficient police force is the prevention of crime the next that of detection of offenders...' this had been drummed into her. She was preventing crime; she was trying to detect crime too. She realised that she had not 'pulled', stopped a car yet, no process, no arrest her record of work would be sparse, and she would have to make it up another night. Kath walked to the edge of the road, facing the oncoming traffic. She peered hard at the tax discs, the seat belts, the lights and even at the A.T.S, the traffic lights, to get her first process of the night...Nothing.

The time dragged on and she realised that it was running out too, she had to get back for her refs, back to the station.

Moving across the road to face the oncoming traffic she peaked at the street name and tried to recall the route back. It wouldn't be good to be seen by the public reading her map book. She could not picture the route back. The more she tried the more confused she became. Oh blast! She moved to the side of the road, propped her back against the door to the shop and used the little light there was to look at her map.

With the route firmly fixed in her mind she walked, briskly, back to the station. For the first time since she had left the parade room and her hot tea, she was warm again. The tea she had made of course, 'plonks were only good for two things' a PC had said, 'tea and…' he had left that bit open. The rest of the relief had laughed, again her face burned with shame. This time the brisk walk would cover the glow as she walked through Berkley Square.

The back door to West End Central police station was open as the Area car had just pulled in, thankfully meaning that she didn't need to fumble for the door code, another embarrassing moment avoided. She watched as the Area car drove to the bottom of the ramp. The driver, an old sweat of many years, neatly swung the car around to leave it pointing up the ramp in case a decent call came in. Decent enough to pull him away from the inevitable tea and card game. There was a turnstile on which the cars could be swung around. But when she had asked the garage hand, himself ex job, he had smiled condescendingly at her saying it had not been used for years. But anyway, no area car driver would lower themselves to use the turnstile.

As she headed for the stairs another vehicle came into the

yard. She moved quicker to the stairs realising that if she did not hurry up, she would end up at the back of the queue and would be forced to pay for the whole relief's tea. She grabbed her sandwiches from her locker and made it in front of the upcoming surge of officers coming in for their refreshments. Ordering her tea, she sat down before the relief started to arrive.

It was only after the third PC came in and looked over at her, talking in muted yet angry tones, that could not quite be heard over the normal canteen noises, that she realised she had made a huge mistake. She burned in shame again, deeper than before. What could she do?

Kath had sat on the card school table, the Advanced drivers table. They would rip her up for arse paper. She had seconds. She pulled her things towards her, grabbing her own jacket, coat, and car coat. Her sandwiches were shoved into her white hat and she balanced her tea with the lid firmly squashed down to prevent spillages in her hat too. Hurriedly she moved as fast as she could. She almost ran for the stairs brushing past the other 'plonk' on the relief as she did so mumbling, 'my turn to relieve the station officer'.

Kath got to the top of the stairs and paused to catch her breath, still burning with embarrassment, she re-positioned her belongings before making her way to the station office. 'Hiya, do you want to be relieved now'? It was sadly too late to retract the double meaning! The young PC smiled at her embarrassment. 'well, if you're offering!'

The hour on the front counter passed quickly, the paperwork and public were quickly dealt with as night duty was not that busy at the front counter, after the first few hours at least. All too soon she would be back outside in the bitter cold. At least she had avoided the comments from the drivers, and she would have a chance to redeem herself if she could. She wrote up the last few lines from the Bail book and closed it. The Bail book was used for people signing on for bail from court, she thought this was an antiquated waste of time and resources to ask a person to come to the station to sign a book. The bail was given at court and conditions were imposed, then these conditions were passed to the station and every day the night duty station officer had to check the book and see who had failed to appear. Occasionally the person arrived late to sign on, an easy body, frowned upon by the team but still, a body was a body. No such luck tonight though. Two had failed to appear, there was lots of paperwork, but no body.

She prepared herself to go back out into the frozen night, coat on, scarf wrapped tightly, gloves and hat on too, she must try to be warm. As soon as she stepped outside, the wind found the gaps again and she started to shiver. She made her way back towards her beat for the night, back to the Park Lane beat. The brisk walk warmed her enough to undo the scarf she had furled around her lower face. She walked through Hanover Square and scurried past the 'statue of a man', often the subject of a spoof call, for the initiation of probationers who were repeatedly called to attend a man, called Pitt and his two dogs in the Square, only to find the statue of 'William Pitt'. Then on towards the deadest beat of the station and the deadest street on the deadest beat.

Finally, she found a hiding place out of the wind but where she could see the oncoming cars, she waited, and watched, and waited, the time passed excruciatingly slowly, and the cars passed quickly, too quickly. She was not able to see any indiscretion that warranted her diving for the side of the road and waving for a car to stop.

She pushed her body back into the gap and she felt she was out of the wind, and just as importantly, sight, of any passing skipper or member of the public. She lent her head against the back wall pushing her hat forward onto her face, and she left it there as if to close the gap even more between her scarf and the top of her head. She blinked several times, each blink for a fraction longer than the last. She blinked again, then realised that just for a second or two, she had closed her eyes. She did not care, she blinked again. Seconds or was it minutes later she opened her eyes, she panicked, how long had she been asleep? Was it seconds or minutes? Had she been seen? Glancing around the street it was as deserted as before, thank goodness she had been asleep for a few seconds only.

Hurriedly she moved away from the wall realising that she had risked a rollicking just for a touch of 'shut eye'. She moved on towards the side of the road and stood just behind the lamp post. A welcome surprise appeared seconds later as her first process appeared around the corner, she hoped it was a 'no seat belt'. Arm raised like an exaggerated Nazi salute she stepped into the road, breathing heavily hoping that the car would stop in time or she would be jumping for the kerb. Her heart was pounding with nervous excitement as she was about to stop a car and speak to the driver, putting into effect what she had been taught all that time ago, weeks back at Hendon. Again, her need to remain dignified overshadowed her need to be safe. But still a part of her acknowledged that she really did not want a bruised shin or worse.

The driver of the Merc pulled up short and pulled over to the kerb. The driver sheepishly reached for the seat belt then thought better of it releasing it again, allowing the seat belt to run back.

Kath went to the driver's side of the car and waited patiently as the driver seemed to take a deep breath and blow away from her as he opened the window. 'Sorry officer, I forgot!'

As she leaned into the warmth of the car, she fleetingly felt a touch of seconds and sympathy, and even considered using her discretion to let him go with a rollicking. But she soon swallowed that sympathy hard and thought of her own wellbeing. No, she needed a process. She leaned in to ask the man to get out. Wow! She received a face full of booze! Kath smiled inside and thought, 'yes an arrest!'

The man's face fell, and he started to get out. It looked as if he was contemplating getting back into the car. Kath thought quickly and reached in through the open window. A risky move if the driver contemplated making a run for it, if he did run for it, she would be dragged alongside the car until she let go or worse. Thankfully, the driver's indecision lasted only a split second and he gambled on the WPC letting him off whatever he had done wrong. He smiled as he got out, going for the charm offensive. 'Darling what can I do for you?' 'You need warming up?'

Unluckily with every word and every breath Kath's suspicions were aroused as to the quantity of alcohol he had drank that night. Excitement rose, this could be a good arrest after all. The driver was soon on the pavement and a radio call was put through to the station to ask for a breathalyser to be bought to the scene. Kath struggled with the police jargon and waited for the ridicule that often followed the probationers talking over the radio, this time she had little to say on air and got away unscathed as she made no mistakes worthy of ridicule. Probationers were not allowed to take out the new alcohol testing machines that had been issued to replace the old ones that were tubes and bags, these were state of the art, they would deliver a Roadside Test, 'pass' or 'fail', and then it was a case of taking the prisoner back to the station to use the new breathalyser machines at the station. Again, another source of amusement was that she was probably one of the only team members who knew how to use the machine as it was so new, but still she was not allowed to carry one!

Kath had asked if any vehicle could deliver the breath test machine and thankfully the Area car had volunteered. The Area car was the car to be on, it was driven by the elite of the drivers, the class one and class two drivers, both were advanced classes or levels, but the class 1 was just that bit better! There was a bit of rivalry as to those who had these different grades and often one or the other could be heard either moaning that they had been awarded the wrong grade as a two, or that someone else should never have been a one. The second person on the car was the operator, in this case he was junior in service. It was considered an honour to be selected to be the operator on the Area car.

As the Area car cruised to a stop just yards from the stranded vehicle, Kath could see the section skipper in the back of the area car. The section skipper was responsible for the deployment of the officers on the shift and was also there to ensure that she, as a probationer, worked to the satisfaction of the inspector. Unfortunately, this particular skipper had a face like granite rock and barely spoke, let alone hold a conversation with you, unless of course you had at least twenty years in the job or you were the van or Area car driver.

Drink drive offences were frowned upon by many of the team, she had even heard a conversation a few days after she had arrived at the station where many of the officers in the station had been in the pub after work and were discussing how many pints made you over the limit. The conversation progressed to whether drink drivers should be nicked in the first place as they were probably just unwinding after a heavy day. As more and more of the officers became increasingly inebriated the discussion moved to more sophisticated ways of beating the breathalyser. Then as some of the officer staggered out to walk to their cars parked in the police car park in Brewer Street the conversation turned to whether officers would nick other officers if they were drunk behind the wheel. This was when Kath had stopped being involved in the conversation, and had made her excuses, whatever her principles were, she did not want to be remembered this early on in her career for

17

being a snitch or even for voicing her views. Kath had been nursing a soft drink all evening, not because of any sense of righteousness, but only as she had given up drink on her eighteenth birthday. A long story. As she lived in the police section house in Broadwick street, she only had a short walk home where her bed was waiting.

Kath recalled that this skipper had been at the pub that night too but try as she might she could not recall what his opinion had been of the drink drive debate, it did not really matter now though as she was committed. One way or another she would either pass up an arrest and get a rollicking for not working, or arrest and risk a rollicking if the skipper did not agree with drink drive. The lesser of two evils!

The Area car passenger, the 'operator' or 'attachment', handed her the machine. The look on his face said it all, 'I have no idea what to do with the machine', he eagerly awaited her to demonstrate exactly what to do with it. The 'attachment' was a posting for a month, it was awarded to the officer with the most arrests in previous months. The attachment lasted for a month and had you belting across the West End and further afield at breakneck speeds to all the best calls and the best bodies. The attachment normally pushed their arrest rate higher on the Area car as they could pick and choose the creme de le crème. This month's attachment, Paul, had nicked so many last month, and the month before, that he had two back-to-back postings.

Kath swallowed nervously. Thankfully, she had been trained in the new machines and she remembered, albeit hesitantly, the spiel, the wording. that she needed to use. Not that the attachment or others in ear shot really knew how the recent changes had affected taking breath samples. Paul listened intently as she ran through the warning, fitting the tube and asked for the sample to be produced. Paul in his keenness, almost pushed her out of the way to see the machine lights change colour. Between Paul and the driver there was little space left for her to see for herself. The lights changed and as she was about to say the magic words that meant she was in the station and out of the cold, the Area car driver, a gruff old sweat, spoke for the first time since he had arrived. 'We'll take this one, get yourself another, plonk'. Kath froze in desperation. She needed this body, this arrest, not just for the figures which were crucial, but also, she was bloody freezing.

Paul looked over to James the driver and said, 'Stop taking the piss, Jim, the custody skipper wouldn't know who was more pissed you or him!' Kath noticed then the reddened eyes, the ruddy complexion, the methodical way he spoke. Good God how could he drink and throw that car around at those speeds? Paul, turned to Kath, 'only fair your work, your body'. She sighed a huge sigh of relief, and the driver, not sure of what was really transpiring, heard her arrest and caution him, before the police driver could work out whether Paul was really joking or not. Paul quickly continued with the banter with Jim, and Jim thankfully took the joke and moved on to grumbling about plonks, prisoners, and property, as the prisoner's car was locked and left by the roadside. The section skipper had said nothing during the whole episode. He moved over to allow the prisoner to sit in the car, and Kath squeezed into the gap left for her.

The trip to the station was fast, too fast. Kath felt her sandwiches and tea slurp around in an unholy mix in her stomach. The body, the arrested person, had turned from a rosy red, to ashen. They both looked relived as the driver dumped them, unceremoniously, at the back gate of the nick. Taking a call on the main set, the car radio, to a burglary on Park lane, on her beat. Damn, she had been on it all night and there had not been anything. The moment she had left it she had let the side down. She would be in for a roasting now, as to why she was off her beat and despite the body, the arrest, the chief superintendent would check the books, and find her 'mistake'.

She walked the prisoner, John, towards the back doors of the station, up the back steps and into the corridor that took them to the custody suite. She had seen this corridor on a previous night. There had been a very violent group of prisoners who had arrived in the back of the van. They were football supporters and had been celebrating on the streets. They had started to fight with anyone they could, shouting, chanting, spitting, and throwing street furniture, and when an officer had turned up to try and defuse it, they had taken a pop at her, she was a Chinatown WPC called Lorna, and she had bravely fought them off inflicting bruises and lumps on them, but they had also had a few goes at her. Her hair had been pulled and her face punched before the 'cavalry' had arrived. The cavalry turned out to be two vans, one from West End Central the other from Bow street.

The West End Central van driver, a grizzled hardened ex-squaddie, had called through to the control room that they were arriving soon at the station. When the vans arrived, the whole relief from anywhere in the station had reached the back doors first. Let's just say, the drivers hadn't rushed to get back quickly, allowing time, just in case, the other officers had gathered there. As the back of the doors of the van had been opened, the bravado of the drunken football supporters had been replaced by pure fear. They were no longer the ones in control with a single officer, female at that, they were now faced with a few more officers, and the numbers were very much balanced. Instead of a hardened tough, single street cop, they had a few more hardened tough street coppers, and they were not in the best frame of mind. Of course, the supporters knew who the coppers were upset with! There had been faces waiting at the door of the van. The canteen had turned out and there were officers in various dress; sleeves rolled up, ties off, hats and tunics left by the pool table or on the backs of chairs to 'welcome' the prisoners, there was even one of the skippers in his running clothes!

The prisoners had suddenly realised that their beating of a 'plonk' was about to bite them back, they were unhand-cuffed, and they were led up the back steps in single file in one long line. The numbers of supporters and officers were the same, but these were street coppers, they were used to going into street fights either on their own, or with only a few others, frequently vastly outnumbered. The officers invariably would come out of the fights with a few 'bodies', and more than a few knocks and bruises, but relatively unscathed, while the opposition more often than not, came out a lot worse. The corridor swing-doors closed and the prisoners from the back of the van were subjected to the team retribution on them as they passed through the corridor; hitting women was not acceptable, hitting a copper was even less acceptable.

The footballers had bounced around the corridor, off walls, off fists, and off boots. The coppers were careful not to mark the supporters faces but left bruises, and no doubt a few broken bones, elsewhere. When the footballers arrived at the charge room they were subdued and sorry for their behaviour, many were freshly bleeding or nursing broken bones. No matter what the court results were the next day, the football fan's punishment had been delivered. It was doubtful that they would be singling out sole female officers again. Maybe they had grown up a bit that night and they had seen that this could have been their sister, wife, or girlfriend.

Kath had asked one of the officers afterwards why they did not wait for the courts to deal with the prisoners. He had answered very quickly and confidently.

'The lawyers are rubbish, to them it's about the law and what the law says, to us it is about what the scum actually did. The lawyers will twist and turn and look at all kinds of non-relevant stuff, we look at what we saw, and what we heard, as well as what the victims said. We don't care if his mum is shagging his dad's best friend and that was why he is upset; we only deal with the here and now. He hit the officer: like a dog after its crapped on the carpet, he needs to be punished there and then, and his nose put in his crap to stop him thinking he can do it again. It doesn't help the hurt officer feel better if there is an excuse like that, it only demonstrates the unfairness of the system'. Kath saw the sense of his argument, but it was still difficult to watch officers beat up prisoners, there must be a better system, but as she was so new, she did not know enough to form a more structured argument for herself or to discuss it in greater depth with other more senior officers.

Bringing herself back to today, she reached the charge room with her 'body' and led her drink drive prisoner into the melee. The stench was the first thing that hit her, she looked around to see the vagrant sat on the bench, and a beside him was a very sheepish male probationer who had bought him in. His reporting skipper would be on his case for that body no doubt, not only the quality, but for bringing him in to mess up the charge room. More pressingly the sergeant in the charge room and the jailer would be less pleased, and that was the probationers most immediate problem, as they would have to put up with the stench until the vagrant was sober enough to be let out.

Kath had heard the rumours of the local van driving along in the quiet hours of the night, usually with a few cups of tantalising heavily sugared hot coffee or tea in take away cups, persuading the more smelly of the old drunks with the hot drinks to get into their van. Once they were safely in the van, they were carefully transported onto another police station's area, not the rest of the C district as they were all sharing charge rooms and coppers, but onto 'A' district which was Rochester Row, Canon Row and even the Royal parks. They were left there, and the van would return to the station, be hosed down and fumigated. Sometimes the reverse would happen and

23

suddenly a group of 'vagrants' would appear in Soho and the tail pipe of the 'A' district van would be seen glowing as it sped away. The moaning would go on for nights until the 'vagrants' went for another drive, then the so-called hilarity would reappear. The vagrants had hot drinks and sometimes even a meal, the officers were occupied in the quiet times, and the rivalry was continued, who could lose!

Returning to the here and now, she thought even hardened drinkers had been known to drown on their own vomit, so the jailer would be checking every fifteen minutes on the smelly old 'vagrant', the male probationer had not made any friends that night.

The probationer was going through the pockets of the 'vagrant', even the plastic gloves did not take away the feel of the slime in the man's pockets. The urine-soaked trousers had their own feel to them, and the stench rose to assail the nostrils of the searching officer and others in the charge room and permeate into the inner nasal lining. The temptation to not search the pockets was over whelming. The slime made the gloves slippery and warm in parts as they found the most recent urine, lumps of dried crap was stuck to parts of the man's back and trousers, as well as knots of something unidentifiable in his hair. The probationer gritted his teeth and dug deep, pulling out soaked notes, soaked tobacco, and lastly a handful of coins. The officer was about to put his hand in again when the vagrant decided to dive for the tobacco that had already been taken out of his pockets and laid on the table in front of the sergeant. In his haste to see his precious tobacco not be binned or placed out of his reach for a few hours he dived, falling over the charging desk, he landed on the charge sheet, empty handed, without the beloved tobacco.

The charge sheets are huge sheets that are different colours depending on where the sheet needs to go to afterwards, the Charge binder, the PAS (Person At Station) the prisoner or the property officer. The charge sheets held on the large metal clip board that held the sheet in place until it was transferred to the binder later on.

The skipper pushed the vagrant off the charge sheet, back into the seat opposite him, then he swiftly rescued the charge sheet as the man fell across the table again grabbing for the tobacco. In one swift motion the skipper swooped the metal clipped board away and up and bought it down with a resounding crash inches from the vagrants outstretched hand. The hand shot back, and the vagrant sobered very quickly and sat very still, tobaccoless and sulking.

Kath gave her attention back to her prisoner and led him to the skipper at the far end of the room. She nodded and pointed up stairs to where the newly approved station breath test machine was situated, the female skipper said; 'Get upstairs I will deal, tell the other skipper up there not to worry as I will deal with the prisoner when he takes his refs.'

Kath was glad to get away from the stench and she led the prisoner up the stairs. This other room was invariably calmer and with less violent prisoners as it was up too many stairs to take drunks and fighters. It was also the charge room for the females.

Kath led her prisoner up the stairs, wary not to be either in front and risk being assaulted, or pulled back down the stairs, or worse to have her skirt pulled up or grabbed from behind. Nor to be behind the prisoner, where he was able to push her back down the stairs. The stairs were staggered and as Kath reached the top of the stairs and she stopped to get her bearings. The noise, which had died down when she was climbing the stairs suddenly raised in a crescendo. The room was heaving with women, all shapes and sizes, all colours, and ages, and in different levels of dress or undress. All seemed to be talking at the same time and all seemed to be very much at home. Kath guessed that they were 'Toms', prostitutes. The noise was almost over-powering, yet it was not violent or aggressive. It was the sound of the women 'banging' away on the typewriters. The sound of the keys strikes, and the return, as they worked on the typewriters and simultaneously talked, shouted, cajoled, and teased each other and the arresting officers or staff in the charge room. There was also a strong aroma of body odours, coffee, and other smells she did not want to quantify.

As she arrived at the top of the stairs, she looked around Kath took it all in. There were several tables bolted to the floor, these were the tables where normally the arresting officers sat and wrote or typed information from the prisoners, or the charge sergeant sat to process the prisoners. Instead, there were two or three women at each table. The women ranged in age, she guessed, from early twenties to an indeterminate age that she dared not guess out loud. But some of the women looked as old as sixty five!

Women were sat in front of either a typewriter or charge sheet, the women working at the typewriters were calling out to each other and to the surprise of Kath were asking for personal details to add to the form they were typing on. 'Josie, you goin' down as Josie tonight?'

Josie replied. 'No, I've been done twice this week better put me down as Samantha tonight.'

'All-right then call it out, date of birth, age, address, you know what to put.' To Kath's surprise they were filing in their own forms to be sent to the criminal records office, in fact they were also filling in each other's.

The women at the charge desks were writing the charges out copying from a plastic covered sheet. The banter could be heard as they decided the time and the location of the offence they had been nicked for that night. As Kath scanned around the room, she saw officers leaning against the door frames, coffee cups in hand, sharing the fags of the women and chatting away to them. In the corner a lone PC sat struggling with the typewriter. He could be heard over the din in the charge room. He 'hammered' the keys while he laboured to type his forms, in contrast to the almost comparative caressing the prostitutes had as most of them touch typed. He looked up and caught the eye of Kath as she entered the room. He smiled ruefully and then gazed across at his prisoner sat slumped over the desk further along the charging area. The gaze said it all she smiled back at the PC as their eyes met again. He had lucked out. He hadn't nicked a Tom, a prostitute, but instead like her a drink driver. Therefore, he was stuck with the paperwork.

Kath joined the queue for the charging. The female skipper, true to her word, soon arrived, and steered to her to one side, to book the drink drive in for her. The time passed as she worked her way methodically through the paperwork. The charge room became quieter as the women left the room. The banter gone, and the charge room hummed as the night swiftly drew to an end. The paperwork seems endless, and the forms repeated themselves over and over again. Name, date of birth, date of arrest, officer's details, on and on it went.

The drink driver had been put in front of the breathalyser in the charge room. He had blown sixty-two and sixty-four, he was over the limit and would be charged, appearing at court soon, and hopefully he would be disqualified. Kath felt no remorse for the man's plight, though his livelihood may well be at risk. The dangers that a drink driver posed on the road had been drilled into them when they did their training. They were shown the photos of the crashes, the bodies in the cars that were so badly mangled that they had to be left in situ until the brigade had cut them out. These were invariably the victims, the drunk drivers seemed to get away with less injuries, not always, she had seen the remorse on the video tapes of drivers who sat slumped, not looking at the camera, explaining how bad they felt that they had killed someone when they were drunk, and how sad their own life was now.

He was apologetic and contrite, yet Kath suspected it was a sham, as earlier in the evening when she had been chatting with him, he opened up and stated that he had been unlucky tonight but usually he got away with it. With this any sympathy she might have felt evaporated. Finally, he was taken to the cells and he was locked away until he was sober enough to be released, the policy was that he had to be under the legal limit before he was allowed out, just in case he went back to his car, she was finished at last. The night shift charge skipper had gone, the day shift skipper said he would check the drink driver for her later on.

She made her way quickly to the locker room. Bundled her civvy clothes into a bag and threw on her civvy jacket. She normally took her uniform off, but she was dead tired and wished only to get home quickly, she would rush home in half blues, half civvies and half the blues of her uniform, home for her was the section house just across Regent street, called Trenchard House.

She left via the back door not wanting to risk being caught by the chief superintendent at the front of the station in the station office, as he would be checking the station books now. She walked around the station into Saville Row, across Regents Street. It had been full of hustle and bustle of tourists, touts, and taxis last night. It was now replaced by the manic rush to get to work of the millions of commuters who were shoving and pushing each other in a race to get in to work, shoving, just so that they could get to work that one second or two earlier, she didn't get that, she loved the job, but she laughed as she imagined trying their antics to get to work. The eagle eyed of the locals clocked her half blues, they kept a respectful distance away, and some caught her eye and smiled in greeting, these were the ones she knew from the day shift. To others she was just another worker, not realising that she was actually going home, and to her bed, while they worked and that she had been up all night.

Kath reached the Section House and said a cheery 'hi' to the wardens on duty, they were a great bunch; they helped run the section house, supported the younger ones, sold cleaning tokens for the washing machines, and basically acted as surrogate parents to those whose families were too far away. This morning it was Derek, he smiled as he continued with his phone call and mouthed: 'Good night?' Kath nodded and did a half yes, half no, gesture and then went on to the canteen. It was filling up with the people either day off, doing a nine to five or with others off from night duty. It was clearly apparent which were the night duty group as they all looked grubby and worn out from the shift. She looked at some she knew by sight a bit closer. They had splats of blood up their sleeves, one a very bad cut to his face on his eyebrow and another had a ripped shirt. She would catch up with them later and find out what had happened.

She queued for her turn at the counter. The surrogate mothers, the kitchen staff, clucked over her making sure she went to the front of the food queue as she had ordered a cooked breakfast. One of the elderly wardens had told her that it was always best to get a good meal in your belly after nights as the fuller it was the better you slept. So far it had worked, but to be honest as she had no comparison, it just seemed to be a good idea. What it did give her was a space, a bit of time to unwind and get her head around the night and she hoped to give her a good sleep.

As she waited the short time for her food, she sat on her own in the corner of the canteen with a glass of freezing cold milk, watching the canteens comings and goings. Her name was called by the staff and she walked towards the counter to collect her food. As she did so the double doors banged back against the walls as two PCs staggered into the canteen, shouting in the way that only those who were well drunk could do. These PCs, she guessed, had been to the 'market', Covent Garden market and had been drinking with the other shift workers. She side stepped them, but not quickly enough, as one breathed over her and shouted in a conspiratorial whisper that reached every alcove of the canteen, 'Fancy a shag darling?'

She quickly mumbled something and got her food, he lost interest almost immediately. She sighed in relief, and then succumbed to her own imagination. If he had lost interest that quickly in trying to get her, how quickly would it take for the drunken idiot to lose interest in anything else he might try at! She chuckled to herself, finished her food and walked the stairs to her room on the girl's floor. Dog tired she dropped her uniform where it fell, brushed her teeth, and collapsed into bed. Her first night shifts were three nights in, four more nights to do, then the dreaded quick change over. She fell asleep.

The tea had gone cold while she had been daydreaming, so she walked over to the kettle in the corner of the room. It was a huge office. As a probationer she had seen the senior officer's offices and had considered them wasteful. This view had not changed, it seemed to take her an age to cross the room. As she did so she could hear the muted noises from the street on one wall of the office, so she paused and looked over the hustle and bustle.

It was so different from her initial meeting with her new superintendent and chief superintendent at her first station. She frowned and recollected the hardened old coppers who had welcomed her to the station. They were grizzled old time coppers, looking back now she saw them for what they were, bullies and bigoted. She had stood in front of them, rigidly to attention, not daring to make eye contact with them in case they thought her challenging their authority. They had her read a phrase from a framed quote on the wall, she had no idea what it was now as she reflected. She recalled the contempt that they had for her as a female officer, they did not hide it, as they were in charge, and there was no higher officer, not for a probationer, the higher ranks were never seen by mere PCs.

She looked back over the street again and thought that at least accessing the higher ranks by officers of all ranks was changed, she was one of many senior officers who had led from the front, walked the walk, and occasionally had an arrest on the way up. The door was closed in those days, now it was wedged open.

Chapter Two

Dry mouth and pounding headache, what a hang-over, yet as she became more awake, she thought 'I haven't been out drinking for a long time'. Then, she remembered, it was night duty. The sun was finding its way through the curtain edges and fell onto her face. She looked around for her watch, 12.30, she had been asleep less than three hours. She couldn't make out what had woken her, then a noise came at the door, a soft tapping. The day shift warden James whispered, 'Kath, sorry are you awake?'

She mumbled back at him. 'Wass up?'

James said, 'You've got a call from the custody suite, you need to take it.'

Kath snapped out of her sleepy state. 'Oh, shit what had she forgotten?' 'Just a sec James.'

She threw on a dressing gown and went to the door. Still apologetic, James reiterated what he had said through the closed door.

'It's the early turn skipper at the nick; he needs to talk to you on the phone.'

Kath followed James downstairs passed a few curious

residents. She picked up the section house phone. 'Sergeant, it's Kath Peters'. On the other end of the line, she could hear the gruff voice of the early turn skipper she had spoken to when she had left.

'Hey, Kath sorry to wake you'.

With her heart in her mouth, she said. 'That's all-right sergeant have I goofed up?'

'No, not really, just a miss communication. You know you did a PNC check on your man last night? Well, this morning I did another, and you'll never guess what? He is wanted for fail to appear. It must have not been on the system last night. Look I know you are looking for figures, I know you work hard, and I have put you down for that one as well. I will do all the paperwork this end for next bit, and for court this afternoon. Can you pop over and do a quick book for it? I can sign you on for a few more hours after this morning for the over time. You up for it?'

Kath was stunned to silence, she did not think it was a wind up, though it had been known that the team did some stupid stunts, but it did not normally involve another team, so she thought, I must trust him. 'Sergeant, you're a star. I will throw some civvies on and be there in twenty. I owe you a drink or a donut!'

The skipper laughed. 'Hey, you've seen my waistline. Just a black coffee when you get here. Pop to the charge room and I will give you the 'gen'. (The police used lots of military slang).

Kath hung up, James had been politely eve's dropping, 'Well' he said 'that's one for the books. I've heard he's a nice fella; he

34

didn't have to do that. Quick off you go'.

Kath ran ungainly up the stairs. Flashing thigh as she pounded up two at a time, the stairs were deserted so her little show had been unnoticed. So, she grabbed a towel and dove into the shower along the corridor from her room, again it was deserted, the wrong time of the day for working, either coming off or going on shift. Quickly donning her civvies and she was out the door in ten flat, glad she had eaten that cooked breakfast knowing she would be ok until she got back.

She dashed through the streets to the nick and made for the canteen first, she grabbed a black coffee and a mars bar for the skipper, and she went straight to the charge room.

The skipper was sat there reading a book. He smiled when she came in and took the coffee, looked a bit sheepish as he said, 'ok go on then', as he also took the mars bar, looked around for any of his team, and sat chomping on it as Kath read through the paperwork. She popped to the cell and saw the man from last night. He looked pretty rough, his hair was a mess, his face looked like he had slept very little. The noises in the cells overnight had never really abated and the constant call for tea, food, and abuse delivered to the officers, as well as rowdy singing, had no doubt taken its toll on him. She spoke through the wicker of the cell and cautioned him, noted his reply, and then went to do her I.R.B, the Incident Report Book, with her arrest notes. The paperwork was completed by the skipper. She wrote the book (IRB,) passed it over for him to check it, and he read through and signed it. As she was new the books were pretty important to get right, she had been given several re writes in her first days on the team, and she was determined not to have another. At the beginning of the night duty one skipper had thrown an IRB from another probationer on her team into the bin, thankfully it was not hers. The PC had gone away shamefaced and had sat and re written the lengthy arrest notes again. There had been no help to get it right, he just had to do it.

An hour after she had arrived at the nick, she was back on her way again to the section house. This time it was a more leisurely stroll back and using the cut through it bought her out in the middle of Carnaby Street. She stopped at the badge seller on the junction of Broadwick Street and spent a happy few minute reading the tourist badges that he sold. She watched him as he traded and watched as he stayed against the wall to sell the badges to the passing people, then getting bored she soon ambled off the last few yards to the section house and waved at the warden. The afternoon warden was there now as James was gone off after his early shift, she would find him and fill in the story later. She glanced at the time, a little after 2.30 pm, she had to be at work at 10 pm for a 10.30 pm start, so she thought of her choices. She had several choices, either go back to bed, have lunch, and go back to bed, stay up and have lunch. In the end she decided that she would feel really rubbish if she went back to bed again, so she had a light lunch while she sat and watched the TV in the resident's canteen.

Every month probationers had CTC, Continuation Training, in the training unit in Beak Street, just around the corner, she was dreading hers for a variety of reasons. She had been told that the staff were cruel and vindictive, the class work was boring, and the exams were very hard, there was also the compulsory physically training in the basement too. She had already started her revision for the exam, she would do a few hours more this afternoon, she would bull her boots, shine the toe caps as well and she would go into the gym at the section house for a bit.

She got to her list. She found the revision boring and bland, just reading the IB, the Instruction Book. This contained all the laws and rules she needed. It was tedious, and she soon gave up, moving on instead to bull her boots, she gave up on the gym and sat and watched the TV in the resident's lounge instead. The clock seemed to tick slowly as she waited until she had to get ready. She found herself dozing off in front of the tedious TV but then waking with a start to see that the time had flown by and she had to rush to get ready.

Shower, ironing, boots, and books. She folded her uniform and walked to work in her civvies. As she walked, she thought of her first street duty course scheduled for next week. She looked forward to it, but it meant a double-quick change over. Nights to late shift, late shift to day shift. She would take her studying in just in case she had time in the refreshments break or if she relieved the station officer again, you never know it could be quiet.

Kath made her way to the collator's office; he was a day shift man whose job it was to update intelligence records and sift through intelligence reports. Every shift he would ensure that there was up to date intelligence for the briefing on the parade.

Kath wanting to see what had happened during the day and also to see what the score was with the burglary on her beat last night perused the reports and the briefing. She quickly took a few notes from the information for the day and checked the name of the shop that had been burgled. It was strange she had walked that beat all night but as soon as she was off it the burglar had struck. It was a clothes shop. The alarm had been activated; a PC had checked the shop and had found damage to a rear door and clothes missing. She mused it was where she had been stood only minutes before she had stepped out to stop the driver, she would take another look tonight.

Kath checked the time and made her way to the parade room wanting to make a good impression on the relief, she would try and get there early. This room doubled as the snooker room too. On her way she patted her pockets: 'appointments', this was what they called the basics that she had to carry with her. Whistle and Tardis telephone box key on the chain, notebook and three IRB, three accident books, three process books and lastly her truncheon. All present.

The women's truncheon was eight inches long, the men's twelve. They both looked very phallic but the women's looked like something that you would find in a sex shop on the other end of the ground in Soho. She smirked to herself that would be about all it was useful for. It was kept in the side pocket of the skirt in a special sown pocket, or in the handbag. Even if they could be accessed easily the sheer size of the truncheon was not a deterrent, nor was in any good to actually use to hit someone. At Hendon one of her instructors had explained that she had never even drawn hers, not for work anyway. She smirked again, the inference was there, yet the job was full of inference and innuendo. Kath had not noticed that the rest of the probationers had already come. One of the ones she knew looked at her and called over. 'Hey, are you going to share the joke or what?' Kath quickly recovered and said she was thinking of the TV, Porridge sketch she had seen in the lounge earlier. The PC content with this sat down and they talked quietly for several minutes as others relief members made their way in.

Last of all came the night duty section skipper. A few steps behind him was the night duty inspector: the governor. They stepped through the ever building haze of cigarette smoke that gradually sank towards the floor, creating a wave of the smoke as they stepped into the room. Smoking was not allowed on the parade itself, but before and after cigarettes would be lit. There was a hurried drop and stamp by some, others just putting the cigarette on the edge of the nearest bit of furniture, some even cupped the cigarettes into their hand and tucked it behind them.

The skipper in a brisk pseudo military fashion called 'Parade', the room fell silent, bar the scrape of chairs, as the relief stood and presented their appointments for inspection, the inspector made his way down the line checking that officers were producing what they should be and that they were not leaving unprepared. It still did not stop the officers doing that, but at least they left the parade room with their appointments, and what they did with them after that he was not responsible for.

There were a variety of different lengths of service represented on the relief, there was also a broad skill set, including advanced drivers, van drivers, GP drivers and the probationers and others not yet skilled. As she looked out of the corner of her eye, she noticed that there were many differences in their uniforms too. The probationers all had bulled boots, the toe caps glistened while most of the others had brushed their boots or shoes, though there were some that had not seen a brush for a long time, these were mostly the old sweats. The shoes scuffed and some even white stained with barely dried water damage. The same with the length of hair, again the probationers with smart trimmed hair, or tied back, the old sweats with hair falling over the collars some even unshaven. The oldest sweats cupped cigs in their palms and slouched as they were stood waiting.

The skipper came to the PC who Kath recognised was the same PC who the skipper had thrown the IRB into the bin previously. The PC had made a good effort on his clothes, eager to please no doubt, the boots were bulled and smart, he was clean shaven, and his hair was the correct length. The skipper hesitated, looking for something to be able to say to the PC. This time there were no faults that he could pick him up on, so, almost truculently the skipper moved on to the rest of the relief. Not even bothering to really look at the rest especially the old sweats, he would be either brave or foolish to take on the old sweats publicly. The old sweats 'guarded insolence' and harsher banter made them a foolish target unless they were only spoken to on a two to one with another supervisor.

The skipper and the inspector sat down and began the postings. Kath expected another posting to the Park Lane beat as these postings were a month at a time. She waited for her shoulder number to be called and she had almost written the beat number before it was called out. 'Kath you're on the van tonight'. She waited for the skipper to make her the butt of the joke by retracting it.

Instead, he said, 'yea good nick last night, drink drive and a warrant too. Ride shotgun tonight'.

'Yes sarge', she acknowledged, and he moved on to the rest of the team.

The resentment was almost palpable as she had been moved to be the operator of the van. 'Tom you take Kath's beat and maybe you can stop coasting and pull a body in'. Discipline seemed unjust and harsh, but the point was made, there were bodies out there and if the 'probby plonk' could, so could the others. She gathered her stuff and almost scurried to the van to get everything ready in case there was a shout. Then she ran back to the canteen in time to get the teas ready. She chuckled inside again, a good body was good enough to get a van posting, but not good enough to get out of making the tea, she had to contend with being a 'plonk and a probby' and make the tea.

A short time later the radios began to crackle, and the jobs started to pour in, the late turn had all booked off and it was their night shift. The control room, recently refurbished, was putting out calls thick and fast; punch ups at pubs, punch ups near pubs, and it was a distinct pattern emerging. There would be money in people's pockets, and a need to spend it on anything that they could, and the West End was the place to spend it with the booze, the clubs, as well as the seedier sex industry.

Simon, the van driver was freezing cold to her, he barely spoke as they put their gear onto the van, notebooks, ARBs, and IRBs, as well as the breath test machine that had been used the night before. Simon sucked on one mint after another as they loaded and then moved out of the back doors and, as the van surfaced from the deep back yard, their call sign came of over the radio waves: 'CD2, CD2, fight at The Sun public house in Beak Street'.

Kath responded to the call on the local radio frequency while Simon answered on the main-set and then hit the switches to turn on the blues and two, the blue lights and the two tones mounted on the roof of the van. They immediately lit up the world around them with blue and red lights and the deep rise and fall of the sirens. In seconds, the cars that had been scurrying around the West End parted and the van took the centre route. Simon often swung the van onto the opposite side of the road as he navigated the series of streets and one-way streets, and in seconds, they were pulling up in Beak Street by the pub. There had been too little time to get nervous as the van had swung through the streets to get there as quick as possible, and as she was either hanging on as the van took corners or checking blind spots, she had lots to do. No police driver would ever trust the judgement of a non-police driver to vouch for the road being clear, or not, as they pulled up or away from a junction. But Kath for her own peace of mind checked anyway, though she didn't call out to Simon to say it was clear. She felt she would be walking for a year if she did!

The vans had sliding doors that pulled back or forward, when the van was moving the doors should be shut, but often they were not. This made for a thrilling ride, as the wind pummelled the occupants, and as the van swerved from bend to bend, the passengers leant over sometimes with their shoulders coming close to being outside the van. When the two tones were on, then the noise was too much, and the doors were slammed shut, it was only marginally less exciting, but it also gave a few spilt seconds to assess what was happening as the vehicle arrived at the scene.

As they pulled up on the scene of the fight both Simon and Kath slid back the doors, the doors crashing into the housing, and both leapt from the van onto the pavement or road. Sure enough, there was an 'almighty' punch up.

The pub was close enough to the section house to consider there being off duty PCs in there drinking, and easy crawl home once drunk. She scanned the crowd, and in the melee in front of her there did not appear to be anyone there she knew. The last thing she needed was a reputation for nicking one of their own, but likewise, she argued with herself, should a PC be that out of order anyway?

The instructors at Hendon had been very specific about fights, unless there was imminent risk of death, wait until there was backup, or wait until it was time to pick up the pieces. Observe and gather evidence, and choose the targets you will nick. Simon was a step or two in from of her, he turned and looked at her and she saw he was cool, calm, and controlled, his face a mask of control in fact. He said: 'Come on stick close. Time to sort this out'. Maybe he hadn't had the same advice she had from Hendon! Then in the background the sounds of more sirens could be heard, Simon must have realised that backup was not too far away.

Kath watched out as she strode into the melee of fighting bodies looking out for wayward punches or kicks or pushes. Simon barrelled towards two men who appeared to be in the centre of the fight, they seemed to have the biggest audience from the crowd too, also the rest of the fights seemed to be minor in comparison. There was blood all over their shirts, faces, and the floor around them. As he reached the men, he growled in a menacing voice that could be heard over the noise of the fight, 'Police, enough now lads'. Through their drunken stupor and flailing at each other something must have reached into their drunken brains, they both paused and looked up, just as Simon reached out with his hands like huge bear paws and grabbed them both by the backs of the neck. In other circumstances it would have been almost avuncular, but with his huge hands wrapped firmly around the backs of their necks, and squeezing, the men both went from adrenaline pumped combatants to submissive in a split second. Their heads dropped, they almost hung like rag dolls from his grasp, they were by no means small men, but Simon had a presence that exuded power and a sense of control that seemed to double his physical size.

Kath reached out, grabbed a hand of one of the men and whacked the Hiatt handcuffs on the wrist before the man could react, in seconds he was cuffed and calm. Kath took him from Simon. Suddenly the calm disappeared, and the chaos erupted again. The contagious adrenalin surge pushed fighters back at each other. The combatant that Simon was still holding suddenly braved up and started to squirm, Simon swung this remaining man into the side of the pub wall as he reached for his cuffs, the man again went temporarily limp as he impacted with the brick wall giving Simon time to grasps his cuffs, in seconds the second man was cuffed. The fight around them was getting more and more fierce. Simon and Kath withdrew from the melee taking their prisoners to the back of the van. The two men forgetting their fight with each other now as they were bundled into the back to await their journey to the station.

By the time that Simon and Kath turned back to face the fight again, having safely secured their own prisoners, more officers had arrived, and the fight took on a greater severity. Bottles were smashed and windows too, bodies were flying around. Kath weighed in and worked with other PCs who she did not know, grabbing fighting people, men, and women, mostly using brute force to subdue them, and as her cuffs had already been used, she helped apply the other officers' own cuffs to the prisoners.

More and more officers arrived from the surrounding stations, C district ones, Vine Street and Bow Street which were just minutes away. The 'A' District officers and van arrived, and other officers too, traveling from D district, Marylebone officers too. Divisional boundaries were forgotten, old scores between teams and moving vagrants between Divisions forgotten too, as all piled in to help. More vans too and soon there were only the dark blue serge tunics and the white shirts of the police officers still standing amidst a mess of smashed glass and pools of blood, occasional bits of clothing, and a random shoe marking the place where the punch up had happened. The radios crackling in the night air with new calls, neither acknowledged nor answered, all around the carnage of a good night out was there to be seen. The rest of the world was non-existent, the battle ground of the pub fight was the simple single focus and the officers had cleared the decks of all those fighting. Their faces a mixture of concentration and exertion while some wore cuts and scrapes as battle honours.

She looked at her watch, they had been there for nearly fifteen minutes. The vans on scene were weighed down with prisoners and almost the whole relief across the three local stations and surrounding stations were there. Still the calls were coming in from the control room, more fights, and more calls. The officers who had not nicked anyone, melted away into the night in flashes of blue and red lights as they left to take calls on their own grounds. The camaraderie forgotten until the next big shout. Kath heard the inspector on the radio directing the control room to assign units from Marylebone and Cannon Row police stations to outstanding calls, these same officers who now left the scene were directed to some of their calls that were outstanding. There would be ribbing about that too no doubt. The section skipper was there at the scene and she saw him approach the landlord of the pub. The landlord looked as if he had been in the fight somewhere, he had blood on his hands and face, as well as ripped shirt. The conversation was brief, the gist was evident; Close up, clean up and come to the station, ASAP.

Then in seconds the vans started to pull away. Kath swiftly moved back to her van and jumped in as Simon swung the van through the streets back to the nick. He took a slightly longer route than normal and arrived second in the queue. The back ramp was full of prisoners and police, yet it was calm, the drunken aggression had been replaced by the drunken over friendliness of the prisoners. The police on the other hand had been cleansed of the adrenalin and were concentrating on the task in hand, to process the prisoners as soon as possible, and to get back out there to take their own calls. Although these were being dealt with by the surrounding stations it was a matter of professional pride to take your own jobs. So, speed was of the essence, and the paperwork needed to be done now the fight was finished.

Officers had low mumbled conversations with the now gregarious prisoners, names, address etc all being recorded. It would be the first of many times for the officers to record and re-record the same details, over and over again. The queue moved forward quickly as the skippers went into overdrive, processing the prisoners, all the skippers were in, even a skipper from Vine Street had popped into the charge room. As Kath reached the charge room, she could see desk after desk full with the skippers hearing the evidence, taking details, and recording them on the big charge sheets. The completed charge sheets were pilled neatly next to the skippers, and the jailer took a charge sheet and completed the cell number and checked information on the sheets. The piles got smaller as the numbers of prisoners diminished, soon all that could be heard was the calls from the cells as prisoners called for a light, a phone call or to each other.

Kath quickly moved with her prisoner to the desk, she recalled what she and Simon had seen and explained to the skipper, that she had nicked him for breach of the peace.

There were only a few options for powers to arrest that were suitable, but with each power there was an unwritten hierarchy. If the prisoner was aggressive and had hit an officer or had refused to calm down after the punch up the charge was escalated, if the prisoner behaved when arrested, did not hurt the officers and in reality, conformed again to the expectations of the officers, they were then arrested under breach of the peace. This was twofold, if they wanted the person to stay overnight and go to court this meant the officer could go for 'court off nights' and have a sleepless morning but get overtime, or, if this was not an option the paperwork was minimal, and the officer could leave quickly. It also gave the charging sergeant the option to de-arrest the person once they had calmed down, sobered up or grew up! Likewise, it meant the cells could be freed up for more prisoners.

The IRB completed, the prisoner searched by the jailer, male, as female officers could not search males, and the prisoner put in the cells. They were free to go and grab some more! They barely had time to grab a can from the vending machine in the canteen before the control room started to call them for the next job. 'CD2, CD2 fight outside the Bat Cave Carnaby Street. Any unit back them up? Estimated 200 plus involved'. A few units piled in together blocking the airwaves. The control room called out the call signs that they had heard, and then asked for any other units, they were all recorded, it may seem pedantic, but it protected the officers on the blue light calls if they had an accident, as it showed that they should have been on the call. The job was crap enough without CIB, the internal police of the police, looking over your shoulder and asking why you went to a call you were not assigned to.

The van left the back of the nick, again hurtling through the few streets needed to get to the top end of Carnaby Street. As they turned into the street, almost opposite the local court, what met Kath's eyes was like a scene from an apocalypse film, combined with a fancy-dress convention. The top of the street was filled with revellers in differing costumes, there were vampires, zombies and many more. But rather than a peaceful party that was the norm at the bat cave the 'contents' of the cave were a flurrying fighting mess of men, women and strange supernatural looking creatures, all intent on bloodletting, the apocalypse was here!

The van came to a stop, and at the other end of the street another police vehicle could be seen. Simon turned to Kath; 'I think we will wait for this one'. Sure enough, in seconds more and more vehicles appeared, the top of the street was surrounded by vehicles. The street was for all intents cordoned off by officers or vehicles. Officers then piled out of the vehicles, and the fighters suddenly realised that their private vendettas were secondary as another more urgent need had arisen, the need to get out, un-arrested and get home a sobering thought for those that still had that ability.

The fighters turned their attention to the police officers blocking the escape, cars, vans, and police officers themselves all created the barrier across their escape route. At first just one or two people started to walk away from the melee, then as they passed unscathed past police lines, more and more started to shuffle past them, taking hope that they were not going to be arrested that night. Unlike the previous fight the police let them through, though occasionally someone would say something to the police, a comment about their injury, the officers could be heard saying 'do you want to press charges, and can you point them out?' the answers were always the same, and 'no charges, no they could not point them out'. Rarely a drunken comment was met with a stern retort from the police officers. Then as the last fifty or sixty left one drunken reveller chose to make the stupidest mistake of the day and called a police officer on the lines an 'effing idiot.

The officer did not need a second invitation, and in seconds the loudmouth was pinned against the nearest wall by sheer strength as cuffs were applied, the Dracula lookalike went limp and gave up without a fight. Much to the amusement of the remainder of the crowd and the police close by, as a dark wet stain appeared in his crotch area and it could be seen spreading down the trouser leg creating a puddle under his feet, he'd wet himself. The fight gone he was loaded onto the van amid jeers and catcalls from police and revellers alike, the shame faced Dracula paired with the stern-faced copper, who no doubt was cursing Dracula and preparing himself to have to search the urine-soaked trouser pockets back at the station.

As the numbers diminished the police got back into the vehicles, slowly the street returned to the peace and tranquillity of twenty minutes previously and Kath glanced at her watch realising it was time for grub. She was starving, needed a drink and a wee too! Simon and Kath were the last to get back into the vehicles and as they had been the unit assigned gave the result to the control room. They told of the number of arrests and that it was now all quiet, no further cause for police action. They drove back across Regents Street and parked the van at the station, time for food and a few minutes break. She almost ran to the loo, grabbed her sandwiches from the locker room and made her way to the canteen, she was halfway through her pile of sandwiches when the radio crackled back into life again.

'All unit's CD and surrounding areas, RTA Oxford Circus junction with Regents Street, persons trapped in an overturned vehicle which is on fire LFB on way, units to deal. CD1? CD5? Any other units?'

The West End had its share of different kinds of crimes and incidents. Ranging from the very occasional 'Domestic' in a flat above the many shops or rarely in the posher Park Lane end richer houses. More often though domestics in the street, drunks, drugs, fights etc but there were several things that were just not common. These were fires, RTA (Road traffic accidents) and death in most of its forms. So, a called that combined the possibility of all of these ingredients had the airwaves blocked as units responded. The scrape of chairs screeching as the chairs were forced back and food left untouched as the crews dived down the back stairs to the cars and the call.

It wasn't a sense of morbid curiosity, or even a sense of heroism that made these people run to the cars to deal. It was just plain and simply that they wanted to be the best at their job, and to do the job that they were here for. They would run to these gruesome and heart rendering calls to do what they did best, help people. After that there was the aspect of course of having said that they had been there, bragging rights!

Policing was different, the experiences that officers had in their careers were usually of seeing and dealing with grief, harm, anger, blood, and tears on a daily basis. These experiences they saw or dealt with in one year of their careers usually far exceeded many years in the public's normal lives. It meant a lot to the officers to know that they would and could do the best for the people that they dealt with. A sense of pride in their work, in their ability and sense of doing a job well. There was also the testosterone filled need to be there and to see the worst! Yet they all cared in their own way and they would deal with the people, and the families and the crowds, as best they could.

The airwaves were stilled blocked, and the control room again jumped in. This time a roll call of those that had to attend such as the inspector and the CID as well as the ground units.

CD1, did you receive; No reply: CD1; No reply.

Finally, the control room paused in trying to raise the inspector, the section skipper called in, he explained that the governor was called to 'special briefing', the skipper was acting CD1. The CID were called and were also on way. The Area car C1, C2 were both assigned as well as foot officers walking the beat on those particular beats.

The odd thing about the West End was that every beat was always covered by a walking officer. It was accepted that it had to be done that way, sometimes the time it took for a car to cross one-way streets and cut through traffic, especially during the day, or before or after Christmas, could sometimes delay arrival at a call. Whereas a walker could get across the beat in minutes. Simon looked over at her; 'We will stay here'.

Kath felt relieved not to attend the crash. This was partly as she was worried about the smell of the burning flesh if someone was burnt and even killed, again this had been spoken about at Hendon. It was a smell that stayed with you, but also, she was a bit worried that she would be lumbered as the 'probationer plonk' to stay there at the scene long after the incident was over, missing her van posting and missing the opportunity to get more work. It may seem callous, yet she had to harden up to survive if she wanted to pass the probation. Finally, the control room sorted the call signs of the officers attending and the air waves went quiet. The Van crew quickly ate their grub, conscious that the quiet would not last long, and they did not want to be belting around the West End with no food inside them, sure enough, the calls started to come in.

The accident scene was quiet for a few minutes then requests started to come in for the LAS (London Ambulance Service) to attend, removal units (to take away the cars), road closures and diversions. But thankfully the persons in the car had got out, although they were injured, they were not dead, the centre of the junction was a mess. The night duty control room informed the despatchers in the central control room in NSY (New

Scotland Yard), and they started putting in diversions for the manic day shift when the road may still be closed.

They had little time to relax as soon the calls were directed at them. They went from small fight to small fight, mostly arriving as the combatants were seen disappearing into the distance, walking away from the scene, usually amidst shouts and abuse thrown at each other. It was now about judging what was necessary. Was it more important to get tied up with an incident that was over, or to be around to deal with fresh new incidents that may require action? The calls gradually slowed down, and soon the van drove slowly around the West End. It patrolled back streets and main streets, stopping occasionally to look closely at a group of drunks, slowly driving past the officers eyeballing them from the open doors of the van. Occasionally the officers exchanging a stern warning, or a joke, with the groups, depending if they were close to the mark and were in danger of passing what the officers' thought was acceptable behaviour or comments.

Then, just as the sun began to rise from the behind the building line Simon steered the van along the last few streets to return to the station yard. Those almost imperceptible changes had occurred in sequence. The late-night drunks had gone, replaced by the cleaners in the early hours disgorging from the night buses into the centre of the city. Then they in turn had all gone now scurrying away to their day jobs or homes. In their place were the day workers, smarter dressed and more confident, focused on their day already, thinking and planning their desk jobs for the next eight or so hours.

The van reached the station yard as the early turn shift poured into the back gate and up to the changing rooms. The unwritten rule was that the night duty was not 'relieved', or dismissed, until the early turn were dressed and able to take the calls. So, as they scurried to dress, the night duty congregated in the downstairs charge room. Talking quietly among themselves, some sipping drinks, some smoking, producing a haze that would linger for the next shift. The steady conversation hum interrupted by the night duty governor as he staggered in. He was red eyed, looked scruffy and unkempt, his uniform creased and stained with coffee and no epaulettes.

No one met his eye. But it was obvious he had not been to a special briefing. It was more likely he had been drinking and had been asleep. There had been unconfirmed rumours that this officer still popped over the borders to other nicks to drink with his counterparts. If this was right, then tonight this meant that he had accrued a vast quantity of disciplinary and criminal offences by his jaunt across the borders.

Realising that it had all gone quiet the inspector coughed and slurred; 'Well done, good work, I will take it from here, you all go home'. It would have been laughable if it was not so sad. He could barely talk and walk, like he would take a call? But knackered and ready for their pits, the team needed no second prompting. They filtered out quickly and could be heard calling to each other as they went to different parts of the building to locker rooms to change and go home.

The early turn governor could be heard chatting to the early turn control room staff, and the nighty duty governor wandered off to join the chat.

Kath was up the stairs, and then into the changing room, changed and away, out the back door again as quick as she could. She knew it was not good to be controlled by people like this, but it was not her fight. She had other issues to deal with, getting through her probation, being a female in this male world and surviving. So, she soon forgot the governor and headed for bed. One more night duty less. It had flown by and the need to sleep was overwhelming.

❋

She ate, washed, and hit the sack. Setting her alarm clock for 6 pm and slept like a log. Kath recalled the way in which she had needed to balance being a female and an officer during those early years. In fact, as she mused, she realised that it was still a balance that she had to control every day of her current service. No matter what she had achieved there were always some politician or private person who thought a woman could not lead this service.

Chapter Three

The room was silent when she woke. It was dark and there was not even a crack of light coming through the thread-bare curtains. The room was warm, and the bed and the duvet had moulded to the contours of her body in the night. She was so comfortable; she was not going anywhere she decided. She closed her eyes again, her brain started to function slowly. It was very slowly at first, then gathering momentum. It was morning when she went to sleep, not night-time. It had been light as it was early spring; the evenings in spring came quite quickly. So, what time was it now? She moved her head slightly and tried to make sense of the figures on the alarm clock. She could swear she set the alarm clock for 6 pm. She struggled to make sense of the numbers, until finally her fuzzy sight cleared, and she worked the numbers. She could see the two, that was strange, then a zero, then in a tumble the last two figures jumped into her head forty-nine. It was eleven minutes to nine, she had slept through the alarm and was due back at work at 10.30 pm.

Reluctantly she threw off the duvet and dived for her watch. Sure enough, it was ten minutes to nine. 'Oh shit', she grabbed her wash things and went to the showers quickly allowing the heat of the shower to remove the last of the sleep. She changed into half blues. Put a pair of 'civvie' trousers in her bag and grabbed her warrant card and money. She had just realised that she was also starving. There would not be enough time to go back to her room after tea, or was it breakfast?

Writing her name and food request on the food order slips she vowed to get a wakeup call from the warden tomorrow, this was too close. She waited impatiently for her food flicking through the discarded papers of the day, old news now. Then, when the food came, she rushed it, not really enjoying it, but conscious of the clock moving on. Finally, she finished her food and she glanced at her watch; she had made up some time it was nearly 9.45 pm. She gathered her possessions and started the slow walk to the front of the section house as others around her in similar attire joined the ad hoc informal conga from varying staircases and lifts as they made their way to work again.

At the front door of the section house the conga starburst and the figures went their different ways to their stations, but all with the same purpose, time for work. Even the potentially bad start could not deaden her enthusiasm and soon she was striding to work and beginning to see, really see, what was going on around her.

Before she had joined the police, she thought that she had seen what was going on around her. Since she had started as a police officer, she realised, that there was seeing and really seeing. What she saw day to day is all around everyone, but people often skim over with their eyes and their mind. They don't look deep enough at, or into, the things in front of their faces. The old sweats continued to surprise her with the depth of their vision; hers, she realised, was developing but not as sharpened as theirs after years of policing. She enjoyed looking as she went to work. She would not get involved off duty unless it was life or limb. But that did not stop her from registering faces, index numbers address.

The parade was held as usual, and the tea poured. So far, the night was quiet, and no calls had come in. So, the team sat in the tearoom chatting about the night before sipping their coffee and tea. Kath listened to the stories of the fights and the arrests, as well as the silly things that had happened. The talk moved to the highlight of the night, to the crash, and one of the old sweats described the scene and the accident.

'It looks like one of the cars had been 'ton-ing' it down Oxford Street from Soho towards the circus. The other car was waiting to turn at the circus and the first car piled into the side of it. It rolled it over and because it hit the petrol tank it caught on fire. The two people managed to get themselves dragged out by passers-by before we got there. They both had fractures to limbs, legs, and arm, I think. The car caught alight and 'tinkle sprinkle' turned up to put out the fire. 'Course the heat melted the tarmac and damaged the bollards but it wasn't too bad. The council did the repairs this morning, but the road was closed until lunch time. The LAS took the couple to the hospital but as it wasn't critical, we stood down and came home.'

It had been bad. Of course, the conversation took a morbid turn to it and the jokes started to come thick and fast. 'What do you call a blonde Australian woman on fire? 'Barbie Q' and so the air filled with small conversations and poor jokes until the room came to a hush. 'All unit's CD shots fired at the Park Lane hotel'. The airwaves hummed with units responding the tearoom emptied and the yard filled with the screeching tyres as the marked cars, vans and GP cars poured into the cold night.

Kath held onto the strap above the sliding van door. The van shuddered round the corners rolling with the skill of the driver, blue lights bouncing back from the shop windows and the sirens echoing across the main roads as they made their way to Park Lane. The van was slower than the cars, not by a lot, but the driver gave way to the area car and the marked police cars, as well as to the sergeant and governor who drove together. The van would arrive and could be used as a mobile station; the sideways seats in the back could be used to treat casualties or to brief officers. Under the seat there were rolls of cordon tape. It was an essential vehicle to have at the scene.

Simon explained; 'The first cars on scene will take the actions and try to catch the person or at least get the description out. The next will try to contain the area, so we will try to get there to them with the tape. If there is anyone arrested, then they will need us too, for transport. So, keep your eyes open en route, as many a body has escaped as the cops all arrive and the villain legs it before they have a description. Look for strange behaviours in cars or people.'

Scanning the local roads, her beat, she searched desperately hoping to see something that would give rise to a stop and the possible arrest of a great 'body'. The streets were deserted though, within a short time the first officers were calling for 'those not yet on scene to stand down'; this was taken up by the section skipper and through the control room, taking officers off the call and redeployed to new calls coming in.

Curiosity makes good coppers, so despite the instructions to the contrary some of the marked cars from the West End nicks as well as any other cars from surrounding nicks drove slowly passed the scene, 'allegedly' on the way back to their patrol areas. The van didn't though. Simon went through the back streets and parked up near the rear of the hotel. He turned the engine off and pulled back the sliding door letting the freezing cold air in. 'You can't see or hear much through glass doors, we will sit and wait for a bit'. Kath turned the main set in the van down to a background murmur and pulled her coat around her tighter and waited.

Minutes passed by. She tried to pluck up the courage to speak to Simon and ask how long they would remain in situ, but each time she thought she was ready, she stopped, feeling ashamed for getting bored and cold.

The units on scene put out more information. They both had their 'storno' radios pressed hard to their ears; they didn't have earpieces yet. They had to put the volume lever between settings to make it quieter, the volume control was loud, louder, and too loud. The storno radio clicked as messages were passed but this was an almost hidden noise in the background noises of the roads nearby.

'Male. IC1, 5'4", black leather jacket, blue jeans, last seen walking away from the hotel, wanted for GBH on staff at the hotel, no firearm seen, but thunder flashes or fireworks used.'

Simon and Kath tensed up as the information had come across the airwaves. Then, as if by magic a figure had detached itself from the dark in front of them, about fifty yards away, the figure was walking across the road in front of the van, head down. The figure walked slowly, staggering a bit. The figure was walking diagonally away from the van and towards the side streets ahead of them. The figure matched the description from the radio. The male was just in front of the van, and it felt he was almost within reach of them. Neither of them had their seat belts on and both were ready to get out and run after the man or drive after him.

Simon pointed to the radio; 'get an active message up, units to close off the area' he hissed, Kath relying partially on lip reading to understand him. Kath fumbled for the transmission switch, depressing it before she listened to hear if the air wave was clear. She let go, breathed, and listened, realising that she had cut someone off. She listened to the transmission, it was a slow drawling voice; the content of the call was mundane and chatty blocking the airwaves. She waited, desperately willing the PC to get on with it.

He paused and she cut in; 'CD active message'.

The control room cut the other PC off, 'All units wait, unit with the active message go ahead'. The PC with his mundane message was back on the air again, he obviously hadn't listened either to the broadcast. The control room called him by his shoulder number and overrode his signal. He stopped and again; 'unit with the active message go ahead'.

Kath took a deep breath and started very quietly; 'CD CD2,

we have sight of the suspect from the hotel in park lane, he is in Grosvenor Street, we are watching him, can we have other units to surround the area please?'

'C1 we will take ...' and so units close by called out the junctions they would take. All coppers seemed to have an encyclopaedic memory for the streets on the ground and any ground they worked on, even on demonstrations you needed to know your environment. Within minutes the area would be surrounded. They would all use silent approach no sirens, no blue lights unless essential.

Simon looked over, 'OK come on let's earn our pay check'. They slid from the van, leaving the doors open, they hugged the wall closest to them as they made ground catching the suspect up. Walking fast they had left their hats and helmets in the car. Risking a bollocking for not wearing them.

They caught up with the suspect as he rounded a corner, still looking away from them; he stopped and froze for a split second and then turned back into the road. The next junction along was a police vehicle parked facing them. The suspect had seen it and moved back into the road they were in. He was walking away, head down so he still didn't see them. Thank God for DM boots, thought Kath. But their luck had run its course, the suspect must have heard the click of the radios on the middle setting as he looked up and saw them.

They were close enough to see him properly now. His hands were in his pockets, the front of his jacket was covered in 'claret', blood, and his trousers too. His face was covered in his own blood possibly from a very broken nose. He was thick set and looked like a man who spent all day lifting. Yet, he was also drunk and unsteady on his feet; he had a beer belly and was soaked through.

Simon looked at him and gruffly said; 'hey you want to talk about it mate?'.

Kath thought the man would go for Simon, who although a big man would struggle until other units arrived, she thought. The lack of aggression caught the suspect off guard. 'You what mate?'

Simon said 'It looks like you've had a rough night, do you want to talk about it? They were so close now she could smell the alcohol and she was close enough almost to touch him. Simon and Kath stopped a bit away from the man. He didn't move. 'You had a crap night?'

The man just stared and then without warning bought his hand out from his jacket pocket. Holding an eight inch blade covered in blood he said.

'Yeah, I suppose I better'.

Kath felt her stomach turn to jelly, her legs felt numb, and her arms suddenly very heavy. She even stopped breathing. Simon, she noticed out the corner of her eye, stiffened imperceptibly, he turned his left side towards the man and his right hand went to the belt around his waist on his trouser leg.

She realised that he had put his hand onto the truncheon in the trouser pocket; unlike some officers he didn't tie the strap around the belt he just hooked it into the top of the pocket. She imagined him just sliding his fingers under the strap slowly as he talked.

'What do you want to say then mate?'

'I had a fight'.

Simon gripped the truncheon strap and slid his hand onto the top of the stick.

'Yeah, did you win or lose mate?'

The suspect looked down at the knife as if for the first time; 'shit, I think I lost whichever way'. He looked up at Kath and Simon, whether he sensed that there was a massive potential for violence coming his way of whether he just had enough he opened the fingers of his hand and the knife fell to the floor.

Simon, still matter of fact, said, 'Hey we need to talk to you properly mate, thanks for getting rid of that, come on and sit in the van, you look soaked.' Simon half turned towards the van and the man began to walk just a few steps behind Simon. Simon looked over at Kath and caught her eye, looked at the knife on the floor and nodded to it. She waited until they had stepped passed it and she bent down and scooped up the blade into a plastic property bag she had in her coat pocket, mindful of the blood and the blade.

The man walked a few steps across from Simon, and in a crab like way they made their way to the van. Simon was unobtrusively keeping the man within his vision but still exuding calm and control, yet peacefully talking to him. They arrived at the van which was going to be a sticking point as the potential for the suspect to kick off had increased. Simon calmly opened the back door and slid in on one side of the van on the side wards facing seats on the left-hand side, the man the other side. This had been choreographed to the point that the wooden partition between the driver and the people in the back protected whoever drove the van.

Simon called over; 'Hey lass, shut the back doors keep the heat in and then put out an update, get another driver here to take the van in.'

She did as she was told, and she closed the door anticipating the suspect to suddenly realise what was going on. His demeanour didn't change as he sat chatting with Simon. Simon still had his radio turned between volume settings. So, she moved away from the van and watching through the front window updated the control room.

'CD, CD2 suspect detained Grosvenor Street, we need a van driver to drive the van in and one unit to travel with us please.' There was a moment of stunned silence then the sergeant came on.

'CD, CD3 show me driving the van. CD1 will drive the car back. One other unit to meet me. Kath is it all Ok?'

'Yes sarge, the man is not cuffed, he's in the back of the van with Simon, he is covered in blood, he has been disarmed peacefully, he has some injuries from whatever has happened and will need to see the doctor for a broken nose at least'

'Good job you two, one minute away'

Sure enough, he was there in seconds, Kath felt a sudden wave of gratitude as he arrived and felt her shoulders drop an inch as she relaxed slightly. The skipper must have sensed that it was a very toxic situation, he just parked the car away from the van, and walked slowly yet purposefully towards the front and the driver's door of the van. He just jumped into the driver's side as Kath stepped up into her seat. Simon without breaking the conversation with the man, leant over, and passed Kath the keys, she in turn passed them to the skipper. The engine started and very slowly, and calmly, the skipper drove the van back along the streets they had rushed down previously. The only loud noises were the rain that had started to beat down on the van roof and the engine noise as the van headed for the nick. Inside Simon kept a constant question and answer session going with the man; not once mentioning the blood, the fight, the hotel.

As the van pulled into the back yard Simon calmly said; 'We're here now, we ready?' The man as if in a daze just nodded. Again, as the back door of the van opened, Simon slid to the doors this time, waiting at the back; 'Come on then'. The man slid to meet him, and together they got down off the van. They walked almost brushing shoulders, as between them their combined bulk filled the corridor side to side. Simon casually pointing out to the male the twists and turns and finally the door to the charge room was opened and they stepped in. Only when the door was closed, and the suspect sat did Simon turn to him and say, 'OK mate I am going to need to know a bit more about you now.' And calmly he obtained the details, name, address and all the time the sergeant recorded things as Simon asked for details. It was hypnotic, the calmness the level way in which he spoke, asking first one question then another. The man stumbling quietly through his responses, hooked to the dialogue that Simon had him in.

The door the charge room crashed back against the hinges.

The noise startling the occupants in the room and the tranquillity was crushed. The suspect's eyes opened, and he reacted to the noise. He threw himself up and backwards at the wall and fell into a heap on the floor. This totally unexpected reaction took Simon and Kath by surprise. By looking at the man now he looked exhausted, troubled, and pissed.

The new occupants to the charge room burst in and starburst across the space immediately in front of the door. Police jackets and civilian jackets combined to make a pile of moving bodies and writhing figures. The fight stopped as suddenly as it started and was replaced by moans and groans as figures were unceremoniously collapsing onto the floor and the uniform jackets stepped back away from the piles of people.

As the new occupants looked around and took in their surroundings they appeared to change and loose that aggressive view on the world and it was replaced by a weariness and fatigue as they realised that the fight was indeed over, and they had lost, and lost again, as they were now in the charge room, they would more than likely be at court too. The seasoned veterans, on both sides, knew the score, the prisoners would be graded as to what charge they would have dependent on their attitude from now on.

A few looks were cast at the prisoner who Simon and Kath had sat against the wall. The blood-soaked clothing, the blood covered nose and face, made for interesting speculation. Did the police do that to this man or what other reason could there be? The prisoners on the floor now forgotten as Simon and Kath worked through the initial paperwork with their man and then Kath went to find the duty CID officers.

The CID were always busy on late turns and night duty and tonight was no exception. They still carried over 'jobs' from the late turn and had hoped that the night would quieten down and they would catch up before the handover to early turn. In contrast to this was also the kudos attached to dealing with a decent prisoner, as well as the job-related experiences that could be gained. All of which were needed for advancement in the CID. To be honest it also meant lots of canteen kudos and chat if they had a decent investigation too.

They came down and saw the prisoner, then chatted with the sergeant. As the prisoner was injured and had to be seen by the doctor, witness statements needed to be taken from those at the scene and not forgetting the fact the suspect was worse for wear with booze, this meant that the CID had some leeway in dealing with him. As it was a serious offence they would investigate once the initial report books, IRB, had been completed.

The CID looked over at the mess of prisoners that had arrived just after Simon and Kath's, hoping they were not in the frame for those as well. Martin gruffly rasped at the officers; 'well are these quality or dross?' Martin was at best a scruffy person, on Nights he looked like he had been undercover with the vagrants in the quiet corners of Soho. The prisoners were too involved with their own sorrows to be paying much attention and the arresting officers were used to Martin and his 'eloquence.'

'Dross mate, just dross, we'll have them out before you finish your next pint'.

The cluster of coppers around the speaker erupted into

laughter and Martin started for a second and said 'fuck you' in a half-hearted way. This bought more laughter and the banter continued between the CID and uniform officers across the charge room.

'Martin you catch anything tonight. Other than herpes?'

'Wooden tops been sat in the canteen all night then letting us do the graft.'

The prisoners soon returned to being the main focus as the officers started the lengthy process of recording details, re writing the same details, over and over. No wonder we had encyclopaedic memories of villain's details, Kath mused, as she wrote and re wrote her and Simon's prisoner's details, again and again.

The prisoners were escorted to the cells by the officers now keen to get the paperwork done while drinking a coffee or three, and then be ready for the early turn to take over. Some coppers seem to run like batteries, on and on, others seemed to run only for the time it took to get them to the end of the tour of duty. These then went home come what may. They seemed never to get arrests that took them over the next shift, they seemed to never get a 'court off nights'. But they always seemed to be in the canteen last hours of the shift or in the charge room chatting.

Simon and Kath joined this merry group in the canteen as they went up to write their IRBs, incident report books. They quietly discussed the content of the evidence as they recorded simultaneously the evidence and step by step, blow by blow accounts of the arrest. Meanwhile the others sat either in small card schools or other groups of officers writing up reports. Simon and Kath worked quickly, neither wanting to be off late in the morning, but also the excitement had gone from the job as soon as the adrenalin had left their systems, all that was left now was the need to be professional, and ensure that this prisoner was dealt with, and they had correctly recorded all the facts. It wasn't their job to judge him, although everyone would offer an opinion if asked. Their job was to record the evidence and then to present it before the court. The prisoner would be interviewed by the CID in a few hours and the IRB's needed to be completed and ready for the interview.

As they finished their last few lines they sat back stretching. They looked around the canteen, it was now full of officers sat in small groups, or leaning on walls, a quiet hum of noise covering the content of the conversations as stories of the night duty were told. The occasional comment, exasperated groan or laughter rose above the rest. Then the night duty inspector and one of the skippers appeared briefly in the doorway. 'Piss off, see you tomorrow'; and the canteen exploded into life as tired coppers found themselves heading for home. Simon and Kath were no exception. They grabbed their gear and hit the back stairs. Passing locker rooms to change and passing the charge room to drop off the IRBs and paperwork to the charging sergeants in the charge room as they headed for the back door and home.

The camaraderie that officers had with each other was immense. They did not tolerate fools, nor foolish behaviour, and within ranks looked after their own. Yet there was an acknowledgement that there were officers who went too far. These officers were not liked, instead they were watched cautiously, out the corner of the eye. Making sure that their toxic corruption did not spill onto other officers' jobs. Once seen as corrupt then these officers were never trusted.

Officers seemed to have an equal balance of righteousness. They had a strong sense of right and wrong, though often it seemed to outsiders what was harsh policing was, in those days, the only policing that was known. There was no golden age. You get the police you ask for; officers were not there to be anything more than the enforcers of the laws that had been voted for.

Kath realised that these things had changed. Accountability had become the watch word, officers now were looking back on their history and wondering if they would be called to task for decisions made in those days. She felt relaxed about this, she knew she was honest and those that she worked with knew it as well.

Chapter Four

Nights would soon be over and there would be a semblance of normality to the officers who worked the night shift. One set of nights a month, for seven nights. They worked this shift pattern, while the rest of the month was a rotation of early's, lates', and days off. It was rare to get, or take a day off, in the middle of the week of nights as it threw the body into such shock that you felt jet lagged for days after wards. So, Aid to another division, or to a particular event such as trooping the colour or football was avoided, unless they required some kind of night duty cover. In which case at a moment's notice, you found yourself parading at a strange police station and away from the team.

As Kath left the section house, she was handed a note via the wardens. 'Grab you uniform and parade at West End Central canteen at 10.15 pm you are on aid to Canon Row'.

Kath had been lucky so far, as she had avoided been called for aid. This would be the first one, and in the middle of night duty. She hurried to the station, nodding to a few locals again as she made the short distance to the back door of the nick and then the locker room. The usual banter from the team was missing as she was slightly later than usual as she grabbed her gear, she was the only 'plonk' in the locker rooms. She moved hurriedly to the back stairs and up to the canteen which was awash with noise of tens of coppers sat around with teas and coffees as the canteen staff looked on in blank indifference.

Kath hurried to the empty counter and asked for a tea. The canteen unlike the one at the section house, was not warm and friendly. The staff invariably spoke no or little English to the coppers, and sometime didn't speak to the coppers at all, just guttural grunts and teeth kissing, tonight was no exception. The cashier was draped over the cash machine. Kath asked for a tea and the cashier grunted, then the charge hand kissed her teeth as she slurped over to the machine, her flip flops sliding across the floor, unceremoniously the takeaway cup was dropped onto the countertop. Kath hadn't asked for a takeaway cup. It was common knowledge that they were used so the staff didn't need to wash anything up. The cost to the police must have been high as teacup after teacup was thrown away. The Styrofoam cups that littered the canteen was evidence of the quantity of cups that were used. The cashier stuck her hand out at Kath, a grunt, which Kath judged to be the amount, and Kath handed over a coin, watching carefully as she got her change so next time, she knew how much it cost. The till was never closed, there was never a till roll, the money was dropped into the till and change was fished out.

Kath turned and looked around for a familiar face. She found a couple of probationers like herself sat in the corner and joined the group. As always, the conversation immediately went to the purpose of the aid and why the sudden influx of coppers. As they chatted and handed over information Kath caught sight of some of the shoulder numbers and letters on display on the copper's jackets, coats, and shirts as they stood or sat in various states of dress and readiness to go. They were a collection of D district, so Marylebone and Paddington as well as C so West End Central, Vine street and Bow street. A smattering of A district, so Cannon Row and Rochester Row who were the hosts.

The informality of the gathering was a surprise to her as she sat chatting. Unlike the parade at the beginning of the shift there were sergeants intermixed with in the groups and not separate or with the inspector. In fact, there were no inspectors to be seen at all. The canteen door came open and she caught a glimpse of the inspectors and chief inspector framed in the doorway. The canteen, as a mass of bodies, rose to their feet. The military traditions were never far away, as the officers showed respect for the rank and stood. The chief inspector looked on, casting his eye over the disarray of uniforms and clusters of coppers as if he were on a parade square. Firmly meeting the eyes of the inquisitive coppers. Holding some for a second or two, nodding to some, making eye contact with many, or all of the officers, in a show of authority that said to the awaiting group. 'I'm in charge'. As drama went, he did it well.

'Please, be seated'.

As a herd the coppers scrapped their chairs and sat quietly. The chief inspector's show levelling the playing field, he was in charge, for the moment they would respect that, but only so long as he commanded it.

The chief inspector moved to the counter. The cashier had straightened up, the till was almost closed, and a tea magically appeared in a china cup. That was power!

He nodded and the cashier made a strange grimace with her face. It was a smile; well, it could be. He reached for his pocket and the cashier waved him away. The senior officers had their own canteen that was set off the main canteen. There was a separate entrance, and they were served in their canteen with china cups and metal cutlery. The senior officers were often seen breaching any form of hygiene, wandering around the actual cooking area, so they could get their orders in before the lowly street officers and lesser ranks. Tonight, he was a guest in the lesser ranks' canteen, but he still had the power to command respect from the canteen staff, and a china cup.

Turning, he headed for a clear table, pulling along the inspectors like a comet pulling along the dust debris. They landed at the table, and the canteen still waited quietly watching the theatrics. He raised his cup to his lips, drank, put his cup back in the saucer and then looked up again.

'Evening to you all' his voice carried well in the silent room and Kath found herself leaning over to listen for his briefing, a little bit sheepishly she looked out the corner of her eyes and found others too were leaning forward. She relaxed a bit. He was good at theatrics.

'Tonight, we are going to be supporting Cannon Row Police station as they perform several arrests in some of the large clubs in their area. We will support their arrest teams as they go into arrest, as well as give cover for any disorder in the streets after the arrests have taken place. There are expected to be about 700 clubbers in the club, and we will need to be sharp.'

He continued with the facts of the briefing, the 'where', 'when', as well as the 'who', as his inspectors passed out paperwork to the sergeants, who in turn passed it out to the PC's. There were a variety of roles, from searching the prisoners, to van drivers and arrest teams.

Kath was tasked with searching females in the clubs under the direction of a female Marylebone skipper. She realised there was no sexism intended, it was apparent that males could not search females, so it was better to work effectively. The skipper, Sue, sat with her group of female officers, and gave them a briefing on where to look for weapons and drugs when they were searched. The team were given the nick name of Tampax three zero, by the male officers, meant to rile them, but the women owned the joke and used it.

The three zero was the numerical call sign for the public order unit, while the 'nickname' was often given to a group of women on a public order serial. Offensive! Yet again, an attempt to belittle the female staff. Kath had come across this type of humour in the cadets. The instructors, and the police officer's she had worked with on relief when she was posted to her last stages of being a cadet, had demonstrated various levels of this type of humour. It was a cruel, sharp cutting and offensive humour. Its use could only be theorised. And there was theory after theory she had heard. Some said that it was a way of shoring the weak link. By being brutal with the internal humour, it strengthened the resilience of the officers, so that they did not buckle under the external pressures of abuse that the public gave them. Others theorised that it was that women, black officers and anyone who was 'different' than the 'norm' were not accepted, and therefore took the brunt of racist and homophobic as well as sexist and cruel bullying.

The tea was quickly drunk, and the teams drifted to the sergeant, who, in turn took their teams to the lower levels of the station. They all collected their gear, not that much more than the usual kit she would need for the evening patrol. They joined the rest of the teams at the back door and em-bused onto the awaiting public order vehicles, the carriers. The radio operators filled the air with radio checks and the night erupted into the sound of the engines revving up. As the vehicles departed, the streets around the nick returned to the deathly quiet, and the convoy of vehicles made their way through the busy West End towards the club.

The people on the streets took little or no notice of the convoy of police vehicles. The tourists snapped a picture or too, the locals mainly ignored them. Occasionally, a more subtle movement could be seen, where a deal or a known person stepped away from the gazes of the police officers. Who, like row upon row of hunting birds, scoured the street. Some looking for arrests, others just passing the time until they arrived at their next destination.

No one would call to stop the carrier to nick a small-time body on aid as they passed them, but, if it were a good catch, they might risk the wrath of the chief inspector by stopping the carrier and nicking a better body. The journey though was uneventful, in no time at all they were parked up on the side roads around the corner from the club. They would stay and wait. The radio chatter died to an occasional comment, and the officers started to cat nap in the back of the uncomfortable vehicles.

In every carrier, on every occasion officers would start a card school. It was, 'what was done' and would probably be so long after these officers retired. There was no rank or service differentiation in these card schools. It was a matter of survival, survival from boredom. It was not long before the school played loudly in the corner, game after game, after game, of boredom busting card games. Kath, despite her best intentions found herself intrigued by the raucous behaviour that was accompanying the cards. It seemed that sly innuendo and sexual references, as well as shouting, calling out to each other and put downs accompanied the laying of cards. These seemed to be non-gender specific, the all-female carrier seemed just as raucous as the male, and the banter just as cutting.

The cards were soon forgotten, and she sat gazing out the window. Slowly her head started to fall against the window, and she fell asleep. She was jolted awake by pressure on her face, and she woke to find one of the other women leaning over her with a lipstick held in her hand. Kath jumped back, banging her head against the window, as she tried to get as far away from the woman as possible. This bought laughter from the bus. Kath embarrassed and feeling awkward grabbed her mirror from her bag, as the other officer moved back to her seat across the carrier. She looked at her face, and there was a half-finished penis on her cheek. Thank fully she had woken in time to feel this happening, yet not quickly enough she chided herself, not quickly enough to have stopped it before they had started.

She quickly wiped the lipstick off her face. Another lesson learnt she mused to herself. Make friends with someone and watch out for them and get them to watch out for you. Or don't fall asleep on the carrier, was as good a lesson. The other women on the carrier had forgotten her already and were either engrossed back in the card game again, or were back to their own devices; books, music, such as the new Walkman were all in evidence. The music was a status symbol, those officers who were always on aid had more money and they flashed it around showing off their music machines.

Finally, the radio crackled into life, to the lay person perhaps a frenzy of messages, but officers were able to pick out the information almost by second nature, and soon they were pulling on jackets doing up cravats and generally preparing themselves to step off the carrier into the night and then into the club.

Sarah, one of the newer officers on the teams, but who had served on another district before this one, was the first off the bus. She walked behind the sergeant and the rest of them followed. They stood lined up outside the back door of the club and waited until the call came through for the officers to go in. Half of the serial had gone to the front and the women were joined at the back by half a male serial.

The radio went silent then suddenly burst into activity as the guv' called all units 'go go go'. The doors were forced open and the officers piled in to the dark. There were bodies everywhere some in black uniform others in their 'party clothes'. The bodies moved and twisted in some ghastly ghostly dance caught in the strobing effects of the light as the two distinct factions moved and gyrated across parts of the club. Hands holding some people, others being searched, even more of them sat watching from the tables and chairs, and even others sat on the bottled filled floor.

The officers made their way to the groups, carrying out searches, and taking details. Questions were partly heard over the noise in the club, some mixing with others to make a confusion of noise. 'What is this powder? Is it yours? Where are you from? What's your name? All the time, officers writing and searching. The noise level decreased as the music was turned down and the lights came on. The mystery of the club revealed as a large room with dirty floors and sticky tables and chairs. Background noise rose as police checks were carried out on computers and the results were given. Some unlucky punters, who had anticipated a great night out, were going to enjoy the rest of the evening in an entirely different way, as name checks came back as wanted or missing. Slowly people were led away, some escorted by police officers and handcuffed, or firmly held, others led to the door and walked away.

The night sped up as the club emptied and the carrier crew returned to the carrier. The carrier was less than half full now, officers who had arrested punters had taken other means of transport back to the nicks that were housing the prisoners for the night. The crews were only dismissed from the club when all officers were accounted for, and all officers were then allowed to go back to the station.

They all collected together back in the canteen, only a fraction of the officers who had started the night. But Kath knew that there would be humming activity in all floors of the building, and at other police stations, as prisoners were processed. The chief inspector strode purposely though the canteen, which was long since shut and the staff had gone home, and as he reached the table he smiled.

'Well done, lots of arrest, and lots of drugs seized, as well as evidence to close the club down. A good night. Well, it's all quiet out there, so finish any paperwork you have, and book off and thanks for your help'.

The canteen emptied in seconds, the governor was almost beaten out the way, as the officers scurried for lockers, then for lifts or mates to walk home with. In seconds only the quiet conversation of the officers writing arrest notes was left and Kath and her colleagues were on their way home. Back to nights properly tonight she thought as she made her way home.

Many things had changed around the way we had dealt with the day to day on the streets. Necessity had driven these changes but also the type and quality of officers who had taken the blue. They were no longer seen as the thick and stupid, the only option for people not suited elsewhere. They were now officers who held degrees, and higher, as well as those who did not. There would always still no doubt be officers who reduced the job to a tool to get money, sex, or control over others. But all the while there were also officers calmly going about their jobs, the real heroes. These were the incorruptible ones.

Chapter Five

Mental health

The night shift was nearly over now, and it would soon be back to the day shifts. Kath had enjoyed her nights so far, but she was feeling weary now. The old sweats spoke of how in their time the nights had lasted four weeks. They often debated the merits of either, a week of nights, against the old ways, of the month of nights. The month of nights were easier on the system as they meant that your body clock got onto, and stayed on, the right wavelength for the duration. Against was that the disruption to your life for a whole month, that meant no parties, or late nights, no drinks before work. Not that drinking before work was really seen as a big no when you smelt the parade room sometimes.

One way or another she was ready to see the day light and to get back to that normality again. She sat waiting in the parade room, her mind brimming with the recent intelligence from the collator's office and the crime sheets. She knew the skipper would go over them again, but she also wanted to have first-hand experience of the detail of the information that was available.

The skipper and inspector arrived, and the room stood

half-heartedly, and even more half-heartedly the inspector waved them to their seats again. The waft of alcohol came in with them and Kath looked from one to the other as to who was the one who was smelling of alcohol. On form, it would be the inspector, but who knows? They sat, and the parade slowly started and gathered momentum, as the information was read out, and the content discussed. Kath was pleased that she had read the information herself, as she was a little out of touch of the previous night, having done the aid. She felt a bit more at ease as she had the information already filed away.

Her postings luck had run out, and she was posted back to the walking beats. But on the plus side, it was in the Soho end of the ground this time, well Carnaby Street actually. She knew that being off the beat was not acceptable, but she also knew, that if you were off your beat in Soho and you were posted to a Soho beat, you would be less likely to be bollocked. It was accepted that the officers could also walk together in pairs in the Soho end, mainly because it added to the numbers, and acted to give the appearance of swamping the area with police. There were also more potentially violent calls to deal with as well, so she might get a body in sometime tonight.

Chris was on the beat next to hers, and as they stood to leave the parade room he came over. 'Hey, walking together tonight? Let's get some bodies in, shall we?' Chris was light-hearted and easy to get on with. He was also quite useful in a fight. He oozed control but in a quirky funny way he also came across as a very serious person. Kath was pleased that he had approached her, and she answered.

'Great, thanks, I need some more bodies this 'nights' been a bit low, cuppa tea first?'

Together they made their way to the canteen, the late turn canteen staff were heard behind the shutters calling to each other over the sounds of the crashing of plates and pans. The relief's tea stuff was locked away and Kath went over and started to prepare the tea, 'plonks and probationers' made the tea.

They sat and talked for a few minutes with the other officers, discussing the previous night, and talked about the calls and the results, as well as other mundane copper chat. Kath noticed that Chris was getting restless and she said. 'Can we go, need to get an arrest in tonight?' Chris almost jumped out of his chair to get himself ready, and together they walked out the station towards Carnaby Street. Kath thought she knew the ground, but Chris was soon diving his head into nooks and crannies, and small entrances, as well as side streets and cut throughs. All of which she noted for the next time, knowing that these cut throughs were great for getting to the urgent calls, just a few minutes quicker, or for picking up the stray arrest for people having sex in the street, drunks, or robberies. Also, there was the added bonus, these were often used by the pick pockets etc and just having knowledge of them she felt gave her an edge.

They soon arrived at the Carnaby Street beat. They walked the road briskly and thoroughly checking the side roads off the main street. Just a few drunks and tourist. They decided to try their luck deeper into actual Soho beats, and they continued systematically dissecting the streets, to arrive outside the section house and the market, and then diving deeper into the seedier area. Kath felt as if she had taken a deep breath just before she entered the market, and as she crossed from the normal parts of Soho to the sex trade, she felt as if she had let it all go out. The noise bombarded her, with music from open doorways, shops, clubs, cars, people shouting and jostling. Despite the cold, there were women wearing very little clothes, stood bored on the street corners, and outside the peeps shows. They looked bored, tired, some looked dirty and dishevelled, some looked like they were caricatures of themselves as prostitutes.

Men stood at peep show and gay bar doorways and enticed customers in, pirouetting as the police approached, to appear as if they were inside the doors and chatting with the bored women. As police passed the doors the door staff moved back to their positions circling punters. A game of sorts, but the door staff were not often arrested. The only offence available to the officers was highway obstruction. The door staff knew this, so they were never still, not obstructing the highway in front of the officers anyway. There were occasions too when the door staff stepped in to help officers being hurt, and therefore there was a professional respect. They were also not overheard to be enticing the passing men into the clubs.

Passing quickly and nodding to the door staff to acknowledge that they had at least towed the line, the two officers scanned the street looking for drunks, drugs, and anything else they could find. They were alert to the smells of the street. A strange mix of smells intermingled together to form the smell they associated with Soho. There was the bakers and the freshly baked bread, the alcohol, and the cigarette smoke from the pubs, as they passed opened doors and the ever-present stench of cannabis, urine, and vomit. What a tourist attraction, and yet tourists still flocked to see the sordid sights.

Chris was talking about the tourists that came to Soho. He was deep in a monologue about the expectations of the foreign tourist who came to Soho expecting to see flesh and more flesh. They, he said, must be disappointed. The streets were awash with dirt and food from Berwick Street market, as well as left over half eaten food from local vendors. There were piles of vomit in corners, and urine streams running from bins and side streets. The flesh on offer was mostly old, wrinkly, and bored. Chris laughed at his own description, and between them they extolled the virtue of a cleaner sex trade industry. Banal and meaningless, yet it passed time, as they searched for the next arrest, process or waited for the next call to come in.

Soon enough the radio summoned them to a side street, Meard Street, where, according to the control room, there was 'a male screaming, believed a robbery'. They cut through the ever-present cars on the road, through the tourists and punters, cutting their way through the crowds, to get quickly to the side street.

What presented itself to them as they arrived made them slow down, just a bit. They almost imperceptibly missed a half step. There, in the street, was an old man, maybe seventy or so, with long unkempt hair. The hair should have been called silver, or grey, but could only be described as 'urine yellow'. It was matted and sprouted from the top of his head like Brussel sprouts. Lumps and clumps matted into one big mess of long yellow hair.

The man was screaming loudly, and at first incoherently. When they got closer, they could make out indistinct words such as 'alien', 'money', and then more screams, and then as they ventured even closer to him it became obvious that there was not just a matter of a crime report here for them to deal with.

Stating the obvious Chris correctly diagnosed and summed up the situation.

'He's nuts.'

Kath had to agree. Despite the cold evening the old man was 'stark bollock naked' and there was no sign whatsoever of any clothes. How he got there like that, or where he came from, was, at the moment, a mystery. They got closer, and the old man suddenly saw them. He stopped screaming and shouting, fixing his eyes on them, and began to wail. This was deafening and as the sound pierced their senses, they realised that he was actually dry crying. No tears just a wail.

Kath could see that there were welts on his body that were red and bloody. There were trickling blood lines across most of his body, in fact in, and around, every part that she wanted to look at, or felt she had to look at. Chris moved to one side took his hat off and started to talk to the old man. The fact that he had made the first move meant that Kath could get onto her radio and call for further information, as well as seek advice from the section skipper or the governor, as to what to do with the man. The skipper was very quick to make his way, and on reflection she thought, it was doubtful that it was him that was reeking of alcohol. She would see no doubt when he arrived.

Meanwhile, Chris was talking to the man who seemed to be calm enough. She opened her pocketbook, and as Chris asked questions, she wrote the information down so that she could check it. Soon they had enough to make a few enquiries, and she quickly moved out of ear shot to again check out the information. It appeared that he was a local. There were flats and premises that were not taken over by prostitutes or pimps, bars or clubs, and there were homes in Soho with a static population. The old man came from one that overlooked that street. At least that answered that question, as to how he got there in the first instance.

The PNC came back as 'known to police' and someone who had 'mental health' concerns. That was a bit obvious now, as Chris struggled 'against the current' to get a story from the man. At one end of the street the van had arrived and was sat waiting. The skipper arrived, and when they had finished chatting, the skipper directed the van driver to open the doors of the van. The skipper walked over and stood beside Chris, they moved back a few steps, away from the man, who realised that they were distracted, began his dancing around again. Kath joined them, and the skipper explained.

'Right, he's got to come in, he has previous for assaulting police, and he also is known to carry weapons. Kath, not that kind of weapon!' he smirked, and she had to laugh which did ease the tension she was realised she was feeling.

They moved quickly to grab him, and he was surprisingly compliant. That was, until he reached the doors of the van.

Then he 'kicked off big time'. The arms wind milled despite the skipper and Chris having them firmly held. The legs went in as many directions as it was possible, including up and behind; causing Chris and the skipper to be bounced off the doors of the van and slam the doors shut. The van driver quickly pounced on the old man too, and Kath grabbed a flailing leg. They struggled to re-open the back doors of the van. All the time he was bouncing up and down and wind milling as much as he could. It was like holding a slippery eel. As he got more and more upset and distressed, he became hotter and sweatier. Their grip was loosened as he pulled and pushed in all directions. Kath found herself grabbing any part of his body. Dignity and prudishness aside, she had to hold whatever she could grab.

They pulled him to the door of the van, and he bounced off the inside of the door as they half pulled half dragged him into the back. He was dumped out of sight now of the public, onto the floor of the van. The cuffs were produced, and the fight continued as the cuffs were added. Chris temporarily sat on the old man and they finally closed the doors. The police officers sat back against the walls of the van. Breathing heavily with exertion and sweating despite the cold night air. They had only been grappling with him for a short period of time but the intensity of it was such that they had to take a breath before any of them could speak.

'God, what a 'Fuckin' nutter' Chris was the first to speak, and he had summed it up politically incorrectly but accurately. The man was lying prostrate on the floor of the van. He too was covered in a sheen of sweat, his chest rose and fell as he gasped for breath. He filled his lungs with air and stayed calmly on the cold van floor. Just as suddenly as he had exploded at the rear of the van, now the fight seemed to have been drained from him and in its place a low moaning which was almost inaudible but nagging and persisting. The skipper lashed out a foot which caught the man in back. The moaning stopped as the man writhed on the floor. The reddening on his back mixing with the restraining marks he had already received, making an array of colours, that would no doubt turn to bruises in the coming days. Chris repositioned himself carefully, yet discreetly, stretching his legs. The very subtle change made it more difficult for the skipper to use his feet on the prisoner, but it was so subtly done that it looked like Chris was stretching and using the room around him.

Kath was not happy, there had been no reason for the kick. It was unnecessary, but she felt she had nowhere to go with it and no way of stopping it. Instead, she thought quickly and produced her pocketbook from her pocket, she started to explain to the skipper the information she had acquired from the computer. Like distracting a naughty child, the distraction strategy worked, and she had the skipper's attention. The man on the van floor was forgotten, and the van driver started the van. The moaning continued as the driver took the back streets to the nick, the engine noise all but covered the moaning until the van finally pulled up in the back yard of the police station.

When they arrived at the back door of the station it was relatively quiet, so they quickly took the man through to the charge room. The skipper at the desk in the charge room looking up, barely missing a beat as he eyeballed the man up and down, ascertained he was naked and stated the obvious; 'nut and gut?'

The booking in procedure was completed. A relatively simple exercise, and he was needed to be seen by the doctor. Then the man was placed in the detention room. The difference between the detention room and the cells was not that much, but it was supposedly a better place to be than a cell. The man had remained compliant all through the process. He had started to shiver quiet violently and he had been given several of the dark blue police blankets. They looked more like horse blankets, than one that a human would use, but they offered him some warmth. He haphazardly draped them over his shoulders and Chris helped him to wrap them around his waist too. He appeared not to notice the fitting of the blankets, but he soon stopped shivering, and he then sat quietly. Kath found him a drink, and he sat looking around the room, sipping from his Styrofoam cup.

The paperwork was finished, the man was in the detention room, and refreshments were due momentarily. They decided that they would have early refreshments, so they sought out the section skipper and clarified that they were able to do so. He agreed, as it did make sense, rather than to go out and come back again. They may as well cover the refreshments time for the other officers and support the staggered break times. They sat together in the canteen, alone, as the rest of the team were all on calls or still patrolling. They sat quietly, for a while comfortably eating their food and sipping their piping hot drinks. Soon the food was finished, and they sat back and started the usual mundane conversations that you have when there are no other things to talk about.

'You enjoying the job then?' Chris inquired. Kath had, by this time already realised that you don't give away all the secrets of your life in these conversations, or you would never hear the end of it.

'Yeah, I guess so, certainly different from civvy street.' 'How long you got in then Chris?'

Chris explained that he had been at the nick, and in the job for nearly seven years. Not an old sweat, but not a probationer, and respected as a worker in that kind of middle service.

'You start to get recognised for hard work now, and they start to give you courses and attachments to departments. Not like the probationary ones, but proper six-month ones. I'm after an attachment to traffic, if I can, then after that to the CID. I will take what they offer me.'

Chris continued with his monologue for a few minutes, and Kath was happy to listen to him, as she learnt more about the workings of the police from these talks than she did from the classroom at Hendon.

Her mind wandered to the classroom at Hendon, and the hours and hours of repetitive learning, star reports and a reports, rote learning, and nearly rote learning. It did not really equip you to deal with the incident earlier on. Though she knew the legislation by heart the 'how to do the job' was definitely missing. She had enjoyed the role plays that they did at Hendon, and they were more practical, and she didn't mind the scrutiny that having the rest of the class and the staff looking on at you afforded you. She felt more comfortable than at a table churning out legislation.

Kath and Chris sat through the rest of their forty-five minutes break chatting. Low key non-intellectual yet interesting chat about the work they did, and how they enjoyed it. It was soon time to leave, so they walked back to their beats together, and restarted the usual step by step checking of their beats.

They started again with the Carnaby street end, which was now heaving with revellers from the bat cave. The crowds were beginning to get boisterous, and the drink had obviously been flowing.

As they approached the top end of the street there was a very loud shout, and then more shouts, that merged into a melee of sound, all coming from the top of the road near to them. They rounded the corner, having sped up a bit, and came face to face with a crowd on the other side of the road outside of the Great Marlborough Street court.

The crowd was evolving and changing as they watched. The outside of the crowd moved in like a tide, as members of the inner crowd were forced out from the centre. It looked like a science experiment with atoms colliding with each other. These atoms though were bloodied and had ripped clothes. Unlike most of the fights they had dealt with so far this week these were predominantly women. But not just women, these were women who considered the cold air a challenge against which they must win. They were less dressed than the average sun bather on the Costa del Sol, well nearly. There was more 'arse and boobs', than most people would find tasteful. They all wore shocking pink coloured 'clothing', and all looked very similar to each other in age. It dawned on the two officers that the group were all together, and they quiet probably on a 'hen night.' That did not seem to stop them, the blood was flowing, and clumps of hair were thrown on the floor, looking like a hair salon floor with multi colour hair, though unlike the salon floor, hair flecked with blood.

Chris was on the radio in a flash, asking for back up. As the crowd cleared it was obvious there was a core to the melee of screaming women. On the floor in the middle were three or four writhing bodies. On the floor there was an obvious 'victim' if anyone could at this stage be called a victim. She was lying on her back, her top broken and her breasts almost hung out of the ripped clothing. These were forgotten, as she was fighting to stop her head being slammed, again and again, onto the cold dirty floor. In turn she was grabbing huge lumps of hair from the woman who was partially lying on top of her, straddling her in a way that pinned her body, but not her arms to the floor. The hair was thrown on to the floor as she returned for more clumps to pull off, the floor covered. This seemed to have no effect on the woman, as the hair, it appeared to the officers, was not actually her own, extensions!

The victim in her drunken stupor must have realised this, as she changed her attack to grab hold of the other woman's top and ripped it off. This parody of a mud wrestle may well have been funny under other circumstances and both women, well-endowed displayed much of themselves for all to see. But the blood and the injury gave the actions a serious side that had the two officers walking briskly across the road.

Kath's mind did a strange wander as they quickly raced, yet with dignity, to the fight. In the olden days they would have used their whistle to blow three times in the direction of the nearest police officer. Useless in this day and age, because of the traffic noise. Instead, the storno radio was used. It was quicker and more effective, and that meant help was on its way. Officers would leave their food, hot or cold, to come to the aid of a fellow officer. And a call like this would have the canteen emptied. Kath smiled to herself, they would she smuttily surmised, enjoy the extra spectacle of the voluptuous boobs on display. Well, she thought. If it got help there quickly, was there a problem?

They reached the edge of the crowd. No nicety now, no gentlemanly behaviour. These hens were knocking seven bells of 'shit' out of each other. Chris, a Rugby player and certainly well-built dropped his left shoulder and barged his way into the first of the crowd. The on lookers ricocheting off his shoulder as he made a gap in the crowd, large enough for them to push their way through. The gap soon closed as the on lookers struggled for vantage point.

Chris barrelled into the melee, and the screaming of the fighters was piercing, there was no let up, not even as he pushed his way through. Kath side stepped the first of many swinging arms and fists as she went to grab one side of the assailant, ready to grab whatever she could, to pull her off the victim. Chris took the other side and they pulled together hauling the voluptuous street fighter away from the 'victim'. As soon as the weight was lifted the victim was up like a cat landing on her feet, she was at the assailant and swung hard and low with her fist. It connected with an audible crunch to the nose of the woman restrained by the officers. The blood splattered on to the officers, and then flowed torrentially across the woman's breasts and then on to the remnants of her clothing. Every time she moved her head from side the side the torrent spilled across the uniforms of the officers.

The victim tried for another punch, but this time the officers were ready, they pulled the bleeding assailant to one side. Kath blocked the blow with one arm, and then stepped into the victim bringing her own shoulder to play and hitting the victim squarely in the chest, flooring her. Kath stepped around the stunned victim, grabbed the nearest arm, and twisted, in seconds and despite the odds, had a hand cuff neatly placed on the wrist. A second officer appeared, and the second hand joined the first. The speed of the cuffing was equalled only by the speed that the aggression had diminished and was replaced by the most aggravating screeching crying from the 'victim'. The unfortunate effect though of the woman being cuffed behind her back was apparent straight away, as whatever thread of dignity was holding her partially into her bra disappeared and she spilled out over.

Chris was grappling with the bloody assailant, finding it increasingly more difficult as she was slimy with the blood and what little clothing she was wearing, that wasn't torn, was barely holding in her rather ample body. She screamed abuse at the other woman and struggled to get closer to her. The other officers finally pushing their way through the crowd. The pink clad, drunken hens had filled the side of the footpath and still screamed abuse, and cried, in equal portions. The drunken melee was soon enriched as first one, then another, bent over to show what little underwear if any they had as the vomited into the path of the unsuspecting public, some hitching up skirts and squatting, and peed. What a night, Kath thought.

The vans arrived and three women were arrested. The officers careful not to put the two women together, even separating them at the station to different charge rooms. The assailant going to the male charge room, temporarily until the female one could process the 'victim'. It soon became apparent though that this was an overkill. The fighting duo were in fact sisters. The 'victim' had actually been accused of sleeping with the assailant's fiancée by one of their friends. The victim had then attacked the assailant and come off worse. Which was when the police had seen the assailant on top. The victim had in fact slept with the man and had bragged about it at the club.

Suffice to say neither of the sisters were happy to go to court against the other, and all cross allegations would end in nothing at court. The sergeant in the charge room had other views. It had taken officers off the street, wasted their time, and had covered two of them in blood. They would need to burn that uniform and it would need to be replaced. The skipper thought that the minimum was the punishment of staying overnight in the cells and then Kath and Chris could go to 'court off nights' with the Breach of the Peace in the morning. This meant over time for the two officers, as well as the prospect of more sleep deprivation. For the sisters it meant their stay in the very uncomfortable, smelly, cool cells covered in their own and each other's blood.

They would then turn up at court and have their proverbial dirty washing aired in court. The skipper was not without heart though, as he allowed the sisters to have police blankets for the night and arranged for their family to attend in the morning with fresh clean clothes. So, they could stand, as if butter wouldn't melt in their mouths, in court as the evidence was read out against them. All that would show of the night before would be the bruises, cuts scrapes and matted hair and whatever blood was not washed off.

Chris and Kath completed their IRB's and they presented them to the sergeant. He looked over them and signed them. Chris had suggested that they write their notes in the canteen, but away from the officers in there, as to keep focused on the notes. He had explained that they did need to be consistent with their views, but it was silly to expect that they had seen and heard the same. It was quiet a new view as until now she had only ever been treated to writing what she had been told to write. She didn't of course, ever write anything she didn't agree with, but sometimes working with the older PCs meant relinquishing some of her own originality and thought in her notes.

Court off nights meant that when the shift finished at 6.30 am, she would be back at the court at 9.30 am. She would come back via the station and see the Court Presentation Officer before she left to make sure that she had all she needed. Kath knew she would be having an attachment to the C.P.O. in the future and it would be great to get an insight into this side of policing.

The C.P.O she knew, was an old sweat copper, usually one who was non-operational due to illness or age. They prepared the court papers for court and they would present the case files to the local magistrates. If the file needed to go to another court, or to crown court, the CPO would be the beginning of the process. All PCs were expected to present their own cases to the court. These cases included the basic ones such as drunk, breach of peace and begging which were two a penny. This released the CPO to deal with the more complex ones and to lessen his workload.

The average case load for the CPO would be in the forty or fifty cases per morning session. He would know them inside and out before court. These were the drunks, the fighters of all kinds, as well as the more complicated thefts and deceptions that seem to swamp the West End overnight. The clip joints, and the bars and clubs attracted just as much crime as a small shopping centre. Then of course there was the Oxford Street, Regent Street and Old Bond Street shopping area. The shop-lifting squad at Marylebone took the majority of shoplifting offences from both sides of the Oxfords Street stores but the others the normal beat officers took.

In contrast the afternoon court, the summons court or traffic court, could easily reach over a hundred. These were the ongoing traffic offences. The ones that the probationers contributed too every day when they were expected to produce three process, traffic summons, per shift. Of course, there was no such thing officially as this three-process rule. It was though an expectation that was expected from all ranks above them to prove that as an officer you were productive. It was the least expected. It was often argued that if you were not able to produce such a low figure you were not doing the job properly. To walk or drive around London and not to see at least three occasions where traffic offences were committed meant you were either lazy, blind or a crap copper.

Kath would need to have the books to hand, to reread them and ensure that all her paperwork was up to date. If you lived far away, as Chris did, then there was little or no hope of actually getting back home, even for a touch of breakfast. They agreed that they would stay up and have a breakfast then go over to the station, then court. They could change their bloodied uniforms before they went over to the station. Chris had a spare set of uniform at work he could change into and Kath had spares in the section house.

They sat and read the morning papers as they waited for their breakfast. Both opting for the 'fat boys' breakfast'. The all-in eggs, bacon, sausage, toast, beans, black pudding, and tea for breakfast. They sat and watched as the night shift drifted away to their beds. The day shift ambled into the canteen and then scurried off to work. Then the canteen went briefly quiet, the occasional person on a day off meandering into the canteen to breakfast before starting their day of household chores, going out for the days off, studying, or other activities. Soon they too would be gone and then the late shift would start to come down for their food before their later shift. An ever-changing pattern of officers, their girlfriends and boyfriends, their friends, all revolving around the canteen.

The time moved quickly, and they were soon on their way back to the station. They went up to the CPO's office, just in time to grab their books from him, as he made his way with the night's cases to the court. A short walk away for all of them, and then they were at the court. Kath and Chris went directly to the cells to see that their prisoners had reached the court. The court was too far for an underground passage, she had heard were in some courts, that led from station to court. It was too far, and not possible for the prisoners to be walked. So, it was a short drive in the local van that ferried all the prisoners in turn from the nick to the court. They were smelly and looked like hell. Some bruised and cut, others still in their vomit or urine-stained clothes from the night before. Some, the lucky few, were in court clothes that had been bought for them to the court. Even with this there was the look of the cells on them, they looked haggard and unkempt, even with their make up or posh clothes. The smell was still on them from the night before, but at least they looked more presentable to the courts.

This 'transformation' was all part of the plan of course. They were the 'not guilty'. They were the ones who were either regular punters, who knew the ropes, and knew they stood a good chance of creating the doubt in the courts' mind that the officers were actual mistaken, wrong, or dishonest. Or, they were the chancers, whose briefs, lawyers, had instructed them to present themselves in a better way to try and convince the court that they were 'innocent'.

They had not counted on the stipendiary at this court though. He was known even to the new officers, an awesome character, he was a legend of massive proportion. It was rumoured that he would walk through Soho on his way to and from work every day. He was familiar with the bars and the clubs, often seen stopping, as he walked through the centre of the seedy Soho. He had an encyclopaedic memory of the cases he dealt with, the premises they came from, and the offences that were committed in the area. Urban legend had him often getting out of his chair leaning over the already imposing bench where he sat, several feet higher up than the rest of the court. He would shout at the prisoners in front of him:

'How dare you suggest that my officers are lying?'

Or other such comments which clearly put him as a force to be reckoned with.

The stipendiary though, was the first to chastise the officers if he had the slightest inkling that their evidence was not wholly accurate or truthful. Throwing officers out of the court and dismissing cases with a scathing chastisement to their incompetence or their alleged dishonesty. He was a fearful person for the officers to present to, as well as a fearful magistrate for the prisoners to be presented to. The in joke was, that there was as much urine on the floor of the witness box from frightened police witnesses, as there was in the dock from the prisoners.

Kath and Chris found their prisoners, 'booked in' with the court staff, and then found a quiet corner to read over their books. All police officers practiced giving evidence at Hendon,

104

they even had a special mock court room set up for it, though it was no way as imposing as the grandiose design in this court room. Hendon instructors took great delight in trying their utmost to make the officers look silly in the witness box. Their excuse was, they wanted the officers to be tough enough for the real thing at court. The solicitors and the stipendiary would not be gentle on them, so why should the instructors?

They read their books a few times; Chris reminding Kath of the standard introductions she needed to give to introduce her evidence, and how to ask to use her pocketbook to refresh her memory. There was no more preparation they could do now, so they sat and waited. The quick cases were on first. The drunks. The CPO, Callum, suggested to Kath that she come in to watch. She sat quietly at the back of the court as the officers slid in making a row of witnesses ready to be called for the lesser offences. The court staff bringing in the prisoners one by one in a production line of crime and punishment.

Several of the drunks had gone by, the ones who had said that they were guilty, the CPO at the request of the stipe giving the brief facts, they were brief! Then Callum passed a book to Kath and said: 'Go, on give it a go, you can do the next one'.

She didn't have time to be nervous. She looked at the book and read through the officer's scrawl, cursed the police shorthand that had her flicking through the book to fill in the details that were all over the place. The officer had put on DDTP, shorthand for Day, Date, Time, and Place. So, she had to look all over for the day, the date, the time, and the place. This meant an almost contortionist grip on the book to hold the relevant pages open ready to deliver the content. The prisoner was put into the dock and Callum looked over and gestured to her to approach the back of the court, she did not even have to go to the witness box, she stood at the back ready as she was ever going to be.

She cleared her throat and waited until the stipe was ready, and the court staff called out the prisoner's name and offence.

'Sir, Mr James Johnson, Drunk and Disorderly.'

The stipe looked up, found Kath across his court room, taking in her smart appearance nervous expression and her obvious newness.

'Yes, Officer the brief facts.'

Kath started.

'Your Worship, this is a simple case of drunk. Mr Johnson was seen by officers last night at 23.15 hours in Great Marlborough Street, W1. He was seen by officers to stagger for several yards, then walked up to the side of the court building and urinate against the wall. The police officers approached Mr Johnson, they said his speech was slurred, his eyes were glazed he smelt strongly of intoxicating liquor and urine as he had also urinated in his trousers (the officers at the back of the room scoffed to be silenced by a glare from the stipe). He was drunk.'

The stipe who had until this time remained very calm looked over his glasses at the prisoner fixing him with a piercing stare.

'Is this correct?'. 'Do you have anything to say'.

Mr Johnson shrank into his seat. 'No sir, sorry sir'

The stipe had by this time wound himself up and he exploded.

'Sorry, you had better be sorry. My court is not a toilet, this street is not a toilet, how dare you, you use the toilets provided. If you ever come up in front of me again you will be for the high jump. £30 fine and a day. Day spent. You, Mr Johnson, owe my court £30.'

Kath stepped back. She was shaking almost as much as the prisoner in the dock. She passed the book to the C.P.O. as the prisoner was led away to arrange payment of the fine, the next prisoner was already at the door, and into the court, a production line. The officers on the benches at the back of the court all slid along as the next officer to give evidence moved into place. A slick well-oiled machine, the wheels of justice at work. The last prisoner taken through the corridors of the court to pay his fine, and as he had spent the night in cells, he did not need to serve the day. He was then free to go. He left the court chagrined and skint, smelly, and late for the work of the day. All because he did not find a toilet on a night out. He would be feeling rather silly for a while.

Soon enough it was Kath and Chris' turn. This was a more complicated case as there were several officers, there was again a set routine to be followed. The first officer would give evidence, while the second officer waited outside. The evidence order would be Kath first, so that any damage done could be rectified by the more experienced officer. This time she went to the witness dock. The stipe again visually acknowledging her newness yet not commentating on it. The prisoners had by this time been bought in, and, despite their new clothes, they looked like they had spent a night awake and crying, red eyed and even the layers on makeup not covering the marks from the night before. Kath surmised that they probably had been crying all night, once sobered, they had no doubt pleaded to leave the cells and go home. The bible was handed to her and she was soon reciting the oath. She planted her feet firmly and began.

'Your worship, this…'

And on she went to deliver her evidence. She reached the end and looked directly at the stipe for acknowledgement that he had questions. Suddenly she realised that she had not done any of the introductions she was supposed to do.

She hadn't said who she was, which station she was attached to, she hadn't asked permission to refer to her notes that she had practiced saying that 'were made when the events were still fresh in her mind'. She suddenly felt lightheaded and giddy, she gripped the sides of the box so hard her knuckles shone white through the skin. She had heard the stipe rip up the prisoner and she steeled herself for the barrage of deserved criticism that he would soon unleash. She noticed that the room was totally silent in anticipation. Out of the corner of her eye she could see her colleagues leaning forward, shifting their glances between the stipe and her. They knew she had messed it up, and they waited to see the outcome. A collective holding of breath, just waiting.

Then the stipe looked at her over the top of his glasses. Here it came. She blinked determined she would not cry.

'Officer, remind me, your name?'

She stammered 'PC Kath, Kath Peters, shoulder number 234 C, attached to West End Central Police Station your worship.'

'Yes officer'. She waited, still gripping the witness box, her arms now aching and the ache travelling up to her chest and shoulders. 'And these notes that you referred to. I presume that they were made when the events were still fresh in your memory and they were made soon after?

'Yes, your worship'

'And officer I presume that they were made with the other officer present who no doubt is outside and has written very much the same as you?'

'Yes, your worship'.

The stipe looked at the defendants in the box and said.

'It looks pretty open and shut to me. You have bought your petty disputes into my streets and wasted my officer's time and my time too. Do you have anything to say?'

Neither of the sisters met the eyes of the stipe, and shamefully shook their heads.

'No sir' they chorused in unison.

'Office Peters you may tell your colleague that his evidence is not required' He turned back to the sisters in the box. 'You are both bound over to the sum of £300. If you are arrested again in the next year you will both have to pay my court £300 each. So, sort out this problem and leave my court. Next!'

Kath realised that she was still standing rigidly in the witness box. The court was silent, then an audible release of breath as the officers in the back all breathed simultaneously. Kath had got away with it. The stipe had been as unpredictable as he could be, and he had spared the 'probationer plonk'. Kath forced herself to release the box and walked stiff legged to the back of the court. Conscious of the looks from the police officers at the back who were eyeing her with the same mixed emotions she felt. Some thankful that she was not told off, others let down that she had not been the subject of wrath, and others she felt realising that they could be the next ones, and not as lucky as she was.

Kath reached the holding area where Chris waited. He jumped up and walked as if to go through the great doors to the court room. The rules were clear, you were not allowed to engage in conversation with the other witnesses in the case. Still, he smiled and raised his thumb.

'You OK?'

Kath realised that she was still struggling with the magnitude of how lucky she was. She squeaked an answer that had Chris looking at her in genuine concern.

'You're not needed' she blurted out.

It was obvious from the stern expression that arrived on Chris' face, that he thought she must have messed it up big time. He started to open his mouth when Callum stepped in. The C.P.O came straight over to her.

'Hey well done to you, that could have gone either way and you did well to keep your calm. Thanks for your help as well with the other one. I'll see you when you do your attachment.'

Chris looked a mixture of confused emotions.

'Come on we need a tea and a debrief, let's get our coats, and pop back to the section house and we can have a cuppa before I head home.'

They walked in silence the few minutes it took them to

reach the section house. They ordered the tea and sat in the side room. 'Well come on then, spill it'.

Kath explained the evidence giving of the first case and the punishment given to the drunk. Then she moved onto the evidence for their case and the stipe helping her through the things that she should have said, and the obvious relief that it was all ok. Chris watched on, listening intently to her story, and his grin broadened as the story reached its conclusion. By the end he was shaking with laughter and Kath felt the release of the pent-up adrenaline flush through her system, as she joined him laughing at the magnitude of her luck. That will be a story told tonight, they both had no doubt of that. Chris left to go home, collecting his car from the local car park, to start the troublesome journey home through the West End traffic, and she went upstairs to bed. Not forgetting to call the station office at the nick to book off duty for her and Chris. Money in the bank, court off nights and a good arrest, no bollocking in court and her first guilty case; what a night! She would sleep soundly today.

Kath had by this time in her career, overseen many high-profile jobs and had many high- profile roles on the way to the top. It was always with a sense of pride she donned her uniform. The days of her probation were memories, yet they had made her what she was. She had taken what she knew from then and evolved to who she was now. She had changed what she could on the way up, and there was more to be changed each day.

Chapter Six

Kath slept soundly and woke again to the sound of the warden knocking on the door, her night-time call to ensure she did not sleep in past her alarm. This time she felt like she had done five rounds in the boxing ring. The combined weariness of the week so far, as well as the bruises and knocks from the previous night had surfaced. Aching and weary she made her way to the shower, standing under the ever-present hot water and soaking away the week's toils. Slower than usual, and feeling still groggy, she made her way to the canteen, food, and fuel, before she collected what she needed for the night shift. Walking slowly on weary legs and hoping against the odds that she would not be walking tonight; she made her way to the station. Passing a few other officers walking in, and again forming this blood flowing vein of law enforcement as it flowed to the centre of their universe tonight.

Changed, and up to date, she again joined the night duty parade. Voices now subdued as the tiredness set in for all officers. Small casual conversations could be picked out while the smoke haze hid the people talking, making the conversations seem unreal and part of the mist. The skipper and inspector came in, not bothering to inspect the standing officers, instead the inspector collapsing into his chair and the skipper taking the parade.

Kath was posted again to the van, the almost tangible resentment from some officers, while others appreciative of the work that she had done this week. Although there were no official targets, it was always a matter of pride to try and out do the arrest numbers of the team who were nights the previous week. She was pleased, she had a few positive achievements, though now her legs ached, and she felt hungover, she would not be happy to walk again tonight.

She made her way to the canteen, along with the other officers, snaked along the canteen line and had a tea as the canteen staff cashed up around them. Then sat with her driver to sip tea. It was quiet outside now, there were no calls, a rarity, so instead the officers sat quietly huddled on tables sipping tea. The minutes ticked away slowly and still no calls came in. The tea drank, the drivers and operators paired up and collected their vehicle keys, and then drove out the yard slowly into the night. The bright lights of the shops and the street lighting giving a false sense of daytime as they made their way onto the roads. The beat officers snaking from the station in a pulsating vein, this time of officers leaving to patrol their beats.

Tonight, there was a red-carpet event at the Palladium, there were officers deployed to the local streets to control the crowds and ensure that there were no incidents. These officers were stood like sentinels on the corners of streets, or at junctions, some facilitating the crossing points, others keeping an eye out for the street traders with their horse chestnuts. Others, celebrity watching, hoping to catch a glimpse of the latest celebrity coming to perform at the Palladium. The usual crowd pleasers were there, and the officers were surrounded by the 'ohs', and 'ahs', of the crowd as the crowd pleasers stopped and waved or posed for photographs at the entrance. The bustle of the crowd calling out and relaying, to those who could not see them, the highlights of the celebrity dresses, or who they were with.

On the periphery of the crowds the occasional tell tail sign of the traders, when one got too close, they would be shood away by the officers, and dejectedly they would be on their way. They would be replaced magically by another who appeared from a side street or from across the road. Gradually getting closer and closer until they too were shooed away. These officers at the red-carpet event did not want to be taken from their cushy role and deal with the hassles of the paperwork for the night, it was too good a number. The traders were happy with this, and they moved off into the night determined not to give up too early as the night was young, and there were still crowds in the streets to try to persuade to buy from them.

A few small calls were now coming out, these were to the beat officers, none were allocated to the vehicles. A drunk here, a drunk there, a small disturbance in Dean Street near the junction with Broadwick Street. They listened to the radio and dismissed all the calls, as not really suited to tie the van up with unless they were called to take a prisoner away. They continued to slowly cruise through the streets around Soho when suddenly the radio static scrunched and a distinct and heart stopping call came in 'Officer requires urgent assistance'

Dean street. This call came from the officer dealing with the minor disturbance in Dean Street.

The van driver, Simon, swore, 'shit we're the wrong end'. Kath realised they were going in the wrong direction on Dean Street, having just popped out from a side street higher up than the actual incident. They were going the wrong way, they had to either go backwards with cars backed up behind them, impossible, or they had to go around and come back in from another side.

Simon paused, 'Get out.'

Kath looked stunned at him 'What?'

'Get out, run back to him I will go and get the van round to you, quick.'

The logic was overwhelmingly obvious, if she got out and ran back the way they had come, she would get there quicker that the van, as it needed to go around the block again. She tugged at her seat belt and slide open the van door in one fluid motion. 'Hat' Simon shouted at her. She grabbed her hat from the van dashboard. Incredible, though it may seem, if she was seen on the street without her hat, she faced discipline, even under these circumstances.

In an ungainly run, made difficult by holding the hat and the skirt, she ran as best she could. Initially dodging through the crowded pavements, careering off dazed, dopey, or drunk pedestrians who were distracted by the lights, sounds and smells of the city's cesspool of flesh, porn shops, peep shows and drinking clubs. Soon realising that this was not working, she shifted to running on the road. She was running against the oncoming cars and vans in the street, it was easier as they were slower moving, she could at least anticipate where they were going. It would be OK so long as no motorbike, or moped, or even cyclist, weaved their way through the street towards her, as a crash would be inevitable and painful.

She made better progress and was soon nearing the junction she believed that the call had come from. Normally the street would be filled with blue lights and sirens but all she could hear over her own laboured and difficult breathing was the bustle of the street. There was no one she could see above the crowd line, no tell-tale sign of the officer. She slowed to a walk, the radio was filled with chatter but none of it was helpful, in fact, it was a drivel of a car theft information going out from the control room.

She was confused. What was going on? Was it a spoof call? A wind up? She walked briskly catching her breath. Simon was on his way, but there was no sign of him yet. Suddenly from the lower end of the street she could see one of the WPCs from Bow Street. She was sprinting up the street from Old Compton street. Kath temporarily distracted mused that she must have run for ages as Vine street was the next ground down from theirs, and she would have had to cross that ground, as well as her own.

They both caught each other's eye, and Jackie the Bow street officer, slowed to a brisk walk. There was only a short distance between them now, and suddenly the crowded street in front of Kath gave way, and unintentionally parted for her. There was suddenly a clear view of the minor disturbance.

There was an officer there in the centre of her view,

surrounded by drunken revellers, his hat was gone, rolling on the floor at his feet. His radio hanging from the cord, useless as it was too far to reach, and all the time there was a drivel of information coming out from the control room blocking the airwaves. The man who had been grappling with the officer stepped back, Kath heard a barrage of abuse, a torrent of hatred emitting from his lips. The crowd joining in the abuse, as the officer struggled to stay away from the flaying fists of the crowd, and the bottles and cups. The missiles thrown at him from close range, some bouncing off his coat and leaving darker stains, as the cups fell to the floor, or the bottles littering the floor around his feet, making it difficult to place his footing. The officer had not drawn his truncheon, but why would he, it was useless.

As Jackie and Kath approached from different sides the on lookers turned towards them, the male officer was no longer the focus of their attention.

The person squaring up to the officer reached into his coat pocket, a slither of something shiny appeared in his hand, it was hard to see what it was. As the crowd became distracted Kath heard the man spit out 'I'm goin' cut your throat' and at the same time he swung towards the male officers' throat. With just the slightest of margins, the officer pulled away, the assailants hand passed in front of his throat as the officer leaned back away from him.

The slice missed the throat and instead severed the epaulette of the officer's coat, it fell like confetti to the floor amidst the debris of the street. Then with an explosion of energy the officer launched himself forward toward the assailant. Now the odds were more even, the crowd had ceased their unhelpful intervention, now the officer was back in control. He drove forward, looking as if he was on a rugby field, driving the maul towards a try line. His body connected with the assailant in the centre of the chest, the air exploding from the assailant, as the officer connected with the force of locomotive, chest to chest. The officer wrapping his arms around the assailant at the same time, combining the impact with a bear hug that immediately put paid to the assailant swinging again at the officer's throat or stabbing him.

The officer lifted the man up, the bear hug squeezing the remaining air from him and in seconds the object he was holding fell useless to the floor by their feet. Mesmerised Kath watched its slow trajectory to the floor. The lights of the shops and street lighting flashing on the shiny surface. 'That officer nearly had his throat cut, Kath thought to herself'. She watched at the metallic object hit the floor bounced once and settled.

The crowd now aware that the air was filling with the sounds of sirens and the blue hue of lights as vehicles approached from all sides. The crowd dispersed, faded into the night, to return, no doubt back under their stones they had come from to spend the night in Soho, Kath thought. The officer, now the reserves of adrenaline-based energy depleted, lowered the assailant and dropped him unceremoniously on the floor. The assailant was no longer a threat, now his mates were gone he was alone, not that clever, nor strong either, it had only been the baying of his mates that had sustained the disturbance that long. The officer looked around the floor.

Kath joined him. 'You Ok mate?'

The officer looked at her, he was a young probationer like herself, new to the team, a very quiet officer, and another ex-cadet. He looked a bit dazed.

'Yea, guess so' he gingerly touched his face and then looked down at his missing epaulette. 'God, that was close'. 'I didn't think anyone heard me put up the urgent assistance, the control room were just not listening'.

Kath thought about that too, what had been going on, where were they? Cutting across the airwaves, the section skipper was heard.

'Any officers with the officer requiring urgent assistance?

A split second passed, then the control room staff could be heard.

'Unit with the active message go ahead.'

The section skipper again came over the airwaves. 'Any officer in Dean Street give me an update please? Is anyone with the officer?'

Simon was on his radio.

'CD3, from CD2, officer is safe and well. One arrest.' He continued. 'CD from CD2 please inform the charge room one to come in.'

The skipper replied. 'All received, CD2 see me when you arrive please'.

Kath looked around and saw the probationer looking for his helmet, and re attaching the radio that had fallen off the coat buttonhole. He was then looking on the ground, Kath surmised for the weapon. Kath walked over to pick it up from where she had seen it fall. The probationer's eyes followed her, and as she bent and picked it up, his eyes crinkled in humour.

'You're joking, he was going to cut my throat with that.'

In Kath's hands was a shiny metal can piercing tin opener with a sharpened pointed edge. They both smiled, but also the realisation that it would still have cut his throat, if it had connected, was with them both.

The assailant cuffed, and cuffed, as he was put in the van and was driven off back to the station with the probationer sat opposite him in the sideways facing seats in the rear of the van. Watching, ensuring the prisoner didn't drop or dispose of anything, and to make sure he was safe. The officers who had travelled from other stations had returned to their grounds having been thanked by the probationer.

As the probationer took his prisoner, and the can opener, into the charge room Kath wondered why the control room had been so slow. She had to go in to see if there were any outstanding jobs to do. As she arrived at the sealed control room door the air conditioning could be heard humming, she stepped in and walked over to the PC who dealt with the non-urgent calls and checks positioned closest to the entrance to the doorway. As she did so she walked past the waste bin. It was full of bottles of different types of beers, on the tables in front of each of the officers was a bottle or a cup, she could only guess what was in the cups, but it was easy to see what was in the clearly labelled bottles. Sat in the corner nursing his own bottle was the inspector. Kath collected the outstanding jobs, asked to be assigned and left the room. The officer may have been seriously injured or killed because they had a drink. As she walked away from the control room, she noticed that the property office door was open. There were no staff in this time of the night, is that where the booze had come from?

Kath caught up with Simon who suggested that Kath do a 'book' to say what she'd seen at the incident, so the officer had a witness at court if needed. It wasn't unheard of that witnesses for the defence materialised from thin air, when no one else had been there, or witnesses who were antagonistic at the time of the incident suddenly became pillars of society and butter wouldn't melt in their mouths.

None of the calls that they had were urgent, so Kath wrote a few lines in an IRB, and Simon and Kath sat nursing a coffee as she did so. Kath pondered as she did so about the booze, the property office, and carefully formed her words.

'Simon, the control staff all had drinks, the property office door was open too.'

She thought if she was factual, then he may not take it as a slight against the hierarchy. Simon was quiet for a moment then said.

'Best leave that one right now, he's OK, they'll get their comeuppance soon enough.' With that he went back to quietly spinning his coffee cup as she finished the report.

They dropped off the book to the charge room and made their way back to the van. They started to work through the calls and the time passed slowly. They said little to each other, efficiently dealing with each report, and then moving on to the next. All the while listening to the radio ready to pick up any urgent calls or ready to take prisoners to the station.

Chapter Seven

The night was passing slowly, the calls were neither exciting nor demanding, and yet they still came in. In between, they patrolled the streets, driving relentlessly up and down the busy streets and even they became quieter as the night drew on, making way for the early hours of the morning. The reports were all up to date and they settled in to park up in Soho square. Close enough to go in any direction if need. Simon started a banal conversation about working on teams, and the difference between this team and his old team. Kath felt her head getting heavier and heavier until her chin dipped and touched her chest. It settled there, Simon looking over muttering 'am I that boring.' He sat listening to the radios and then slowly started the van moving again to relentlessly patrol the streets. He did not mind her getting some shut eye, she had worked hard this week. A busy week. His thoughts turned inwards to the control room staff and the property office.

That was a hard one, there was a strong sense of camaraderie in the police, like the army he had come from, it was the sense of being in a community that most others did not understand and did not have to live with the stigma attached to it. He thought of the times that he had not said what he did for a living, not wanting to be singled out.

As the van turned into a backstreet behind the police section house, he just caught a glimpse of a figure by the side of parked cars. His thoughts forgotten, he nudged Kath, making a 'shh' as she stirred and burst wide awake. He pointed over to the figure who had his back to them. Glancing around Simon was aware that he was in a big bright white van with police on it, yet the person had not seen them. He pulled into a space between cars and a van on the side of the road, temporarily obscuring the van from the figures sight and the figure from the officers' sight. He waited for a gap in transmission on the radio and quietly asked if there was a plain clothes observer on the Area car tonight. The plain clothes observer was another attachment, or posting, for officers who had worked hard or were friendly with the skipper. They sat in the back of the area car attending all the good calls getting out and joining in or 'plotting up' on suspicious activity. This was a great way to get the drug deals, the clippers, or the Toms.

The Area car just one street away, the observer was dropped off at the top of the street and Kath and Simon watched as he made his way towards a doorway. The officers having a clear sight of the figure who had now moved further down the parked cars away from the van. The observer stood in a doorway and appeared at the entrance, then disappeared into the shadows. Kath could just see the figure as he went to the next car. The routine seemed to be look around, peer into the rear of the car hunching over to press against the window, peer into the front of the car, again peering up close to the car window. Simultaneously his hand reached to the door handle and could be seen to try the door handle.

Kath's heartbeat quickened, jobs like there were few and far between, hard to prove but a great sense of success as these were the scourge of the West End. The cars parked by punters or residents alike were often targeted by travelling thieves stealing from the cars, smashing windows, and leaving a trail of destruction, insurance claims and embarrassed officers who tried hard to police their beats with zero crime.

Kath had seen him try two cars now, he moved onto the third. The same pattern. This time after the door handle was tried there was a subtle difference to the demeanour of the figure. The back straightened, he rotated and looked all around him, up and down the street. Peering over the car and then with little warning the swing of an arm which connected with the front nearside window. The sound loud against the quiet of the side street. The figure looked around and the light reflected on his face as looked up the street towards the van. Still, he had not seen them.

The observer clicked his radio three times, paused three more. He was moving off from his hiding place. The observer faking a drunken stagger and slowly staggering from the doorway, adjusting his trousers as if he had been peeing in the doorway. The figure dismissed him as inconsequential, and then with a sharp movement cleared any remaining glass form the window.

Police liked to catch these thieves before the damage was done but realised that the proof that was required was ridiculous. In this case there had not been the ability to prevent the criminal damage, instead the figure had committed the substantive offence making proving it much easier.

The figure grabbed a brief case from the front seat of the car, straightening, he suddenly went from a cautious figure in the shadows to a confident businessperson on his way home carrying his work briefcase. The figure started to walk away from the van, the observer slightly ahead of him on the other side of the road, still staggering slightly, and bouncing off cars. The observer stumbled between the cars and onto the road that had separated them, still causing little consternation to the thief. The angle increased and the observer was gradually reaching the other side of the street. Kath and Simon, who had slipped off their seat belts and had the engine running slowly, pulled away from the kerb into the main part of the street, partially separated from view by the parked vehicles.

The radio clicked twice, then twice more. Simon accelerated towards the back of the figure as simultaneously the observer straightened up and became a sober figure blocking the path of the thief from the front. The observer was not a small person, in fact hardly any police officers were, as the minimum height requirement was 5'10" for men. He was like a brick wall in the path of the thief, who decided he would hold onto briefcase, turn, and run back the way he had come. As he turned, the van slammed on its brakes, halting in the centre of the road. Kath bounded out, again skirt flailing in the jump from the vans high seat, she ran to cut off the escape along the footpath. Simon jumping from the other side to run around the front of the van. The figure was trapped.

Slowly, he bent forward, and apparently went to place the brief case on the floor, in a sudden shift he straightened and threw the brief case high into the air, to go over the gate to his side. This was closely followed by a sprint at Kath along the pavement. Kath was running towards him, she steeled herself, she was not going to let this one get away. He ran at her, his legs pumping as he tried to gather speed. Kath kept going, realising that it was going to be a test of nerves as well as physicality. The figure reached out an arm to push her aside, as if handing off in a rugby game, Kath took the opportunity to grab the arm wrapping both her hands around it and immediately acted as an anchor stopping the figure from running, instead colliding with her with a force that temporarily knocked the air from her lungs. Yet she still hung on as he tried to pull his arm free, punching the hands that held it tightly. Then in desperation kicking out at her connecting with her shins.

Out of the melee of flailing arms she saw both Simon and the observer arrive. The flaying stopped as Simon and the observer grabbed the figure's arms and with a short sharp cuff across the back of the head the figure realised that he was beaten. The man was pinned, the car was clearly smashed and had been seen. Bang to rights, there was only the necessity to get the brief case back. Suddenly slowly the large gate beside them opened and a head peered out.

'Hiya Kath, you need this?'

The brief case had landed in the rear car park of the section house, and the warden had been doing the security checks had seen it go over and heard the arrest. The evidence was all there.

The observer melted back into the night, grabbing a lift back to the station in the Area car, rather than spend too much time face to face with the thief, just in case he may be up the West End again. The thief was placed in the van, handcuffed, and Simon drove the van back to the station. This would keep Kath occupied for hours. Simon would quickly write up his book, and 'go witness', then he would pick up a walker to keep the van on the road, it was too valuable a commodity to tie up at the station. Likewise, the observer would do his book, go down as a witness, but as he had seen more than Simon he would stay and do a more thorough book, as well as share the paperwork.

The prisoner was taken to the station and booked in very quickly, and Kath spent a little time writing up a book to make sure that the book contained all the evidence that was required. Kath had to explain in the book that she had at some point lost sight off the prisoner just before he smashed the window. This enabled her to think more clearly about the evidence that she had seen, and how the evidential threshold was met. Kath quickly completed the paperwork typing numerous times the prisoners name, address, date of birth, over, and over, and over, again. She continued to have the radio on and to listen to the radio calls that were coming out. None of them was significant and none of them required further assistance from the officers doing the paperwork. Finally, the paperwork was finished, the prisoner was booked in for the night. Kath could grab a cup of tea before she spoke to the section sergeant to ask what she should do now that she had finished.

It was not quite time to go off duty, yet it would almost be pointless to do any patrolling, other than the beat around the station, which to put it mildly was boring. She was just about to step from the charge room on the ground floor, to the front office, when she caught sight of a tall man in a suit, as he entered the station office from the far side. There was no station officer in sight, the property office door was still ajar, and she was sure the bottles were still in the waste bin in the control room. She was trapped in the charge room; the suited man was the superintendent of their station. He frequently checked the 'books' in the early hours, as did the chief super as well.

The books consisted of the books that were needed in the station office. These included the OB; the Occurrence Book, where anything that was important was recorded such as Sudden Deaths and fires. There was a plethora of property books such as the book 66-property suspected to be involved in crime, as well as lost property and property found. Persons at station-those arrested and not charged. Each were usually piled up, ruled off dated and timed, and ready for inspection. The station officer was not there, there were no books, and the superintendent was standing by the station desk. He was between her and the control room. She could not warn them on the radio as there was always a radio handset on the station officers' desk so they could hear what was happening as well as put out information.

Kath turned to the charge room skipper and jailer as she stepped hurriedly out of the sight of the window. She mouthed 'Super is in'. The jailer grabbed his tie which was hanging off his epaulette and quickly fixed it in place. He almost ran down the cells to check that the prisoners were all alive, then back to the charge sheets to make sure that everything he was responsible for was up to date. The skipper too grabbed the charge books, PAS binder and flicked through them ensuring that all entries were up to date. All that appeared to be missing was the outstanding property to be booked in. This was not an issue as it was all spread over the table to be checked before the early turn took over. Kath helped where she could, bagging and writing labels, and minutes ticked by. There was no sound from the front office, none of them dared to look around the door in case the super saw them.

Then from the back of the station came a raucous cacophony of noise. It was singing, and voices shouting in banter, and the sound of something being dragged. At first Kath thought it was a prisoner. Then she recognised the voices, the governor, the PC from the front counter and others. As they drew level with the charge room door that looked on the main corridor the skipper waved frantically to them that the super was in the station office. It was too late, the noised had preceded them. The super was on his feet, timed to perfection, he stepped out from the station office into the corridor and stood taking in all the imperfection in his 'should be perfect' station. Kath, the jailer, and the skipper sidled to the side door and peered through the glass window.

In front of the super was a huddle of semi uniformed officers in various attire. The common thing was, they were all drunk or had been drinking. They were pushing and pulling large boxes of beer along the floor towards the station office, and the property office. The beer was in torn open exhibit bags, bags that were obviously meant for a larger cargo, the contents now looking inconsequential in the overly large bags.

The officers stopped. The inspector belched and the super stared incredulously at them. Second's past and neither moved. Kath realised that she and the skipper and jailer were all holding their collective breaths, as almost comically they all exhaled together. The super finally spoke.

'Right, the four of you, pull that into the station office. Tidy yourselves up and report to my office in ten minutes, in full uniform!'

There was no hiding the steel in the stern expression. The words delivered with the power of a person who knew his place in the world and expected to be obeyed.

'Bring your pocketbooks.'

This last reference was that disciplinary process was about to take place.

In silence the officers pulled the bags into the station office, bewildered they almost staggered/ran away to find the various bits of uniform to parade in the super's office. The super did an almost full turn on his heel surveying the Station office. He took in the lack of books for him to check. The person stood at the front counter waiting for service, the now open door to the control room, and therefore the full view of the waste bin full of beer bottles. It would have been useless to try to hide them as there were so many and there were no places to hide them anyway. The fumes no doubt that were being escaping would have given the game away anyway. Also, taking in the three over watchers at the glass window of the charge room.

'You, come here.' Kath jumped and stumbled through the doorway. Racking her brain for anything she had done wrong.

'Take over the station office.' Turning to the skipper and jailer he said.

'Right, help her to count these up. I want a cross reference of what is missing as soon as possible. Collect all the beer bottles etc from in there' he gestured to the control room 'I want to know if they are the same as these and I want a tally of them too. Get the section skipper in to take over your prisoners'.

Stunned, they quickly moved into the station office. Kath, to deal with the person at the counter. The jailer, to grab the property books from the property office to be able to check off the missing beers, and the skipper to the control room to grab the waste bin full of booze. The three had no choice, they could not disobey a direct order, even if they had wanted to, and the other officers had to see it that way. A silence descended on the control room as the bottles were bought out and matched against the missing booze.

The control staff were obviously aware that they were in the shit too. The question was, how deep, and how many of them. The radios still crackled with a minimal traffic that was expected of the earliest part of the morning. The streets outside again changed from tourists and soho visitors, to cleaners, to early morning workers, the subtle changing to the day workers who took over filling the transport and the roads. The early turn staff began to arrive.

It seems that messages can be passed through the ether, as officers from the early turn came in, they were subdued and watchful. Quietly going about the morning routines, immaculately attired, and voices at a minimal they went about their business as usual. Kath, the night duty jailer and the night duty charging skipper all sat or stood around the charge room desks. The bottles and bags moved to a more convenient height. There were two distinct batches of almost identical bottles. On one side the full ones packed in a cardboard crate, the other the empty ones. In between a raft a paperwork and the evidence that would be enough to discipline the officers for several offences including possible criminal charges too. The paperwork had been retrieved and the calculations made. There were over half of the original bottles of beers missing from the property bags, numbering in the tens, all the product of a raid on a local club.

The three stood looking at the bottles in silence. Suddenly the loud ring of the charge room phone pierced their silence, making them all start. They looked from one to another as the skipper hesitantly lifted the receiver, making eye contact with them both in turn. 'Charge room, West End Central'. They could not hear the content of the call, but the tone was clear as was the caller's voice. The skipper made several statements of affirmation followed by 'sir'. This left them in no doubt as to the identity of the caller. Then the skipper laid out the numerical discrepancy to the superintendent and clarified it was the same batch. He listened a few seconds more then said 'sir' and hung up. He was ashen.

'We need to re-bag these from the raid, then we need to bag the empties. They will be used as evidence, so they need to be entered properly. The superintendent has called in CIB2 and they are on their way. They will take over, he needs a statement from us all to say we have done this and what we found, then we can go off duty.'

Regardless of their feelings the three had been pulled into the mess that part of the team had created. They were involved, whether they liked it or not, and they would be part of the discipline or worse. The prospect of giving evidence against a colleague was pretty awful, against their own team, was devastating. Even though it had no doubt not crossed the minds of the officers who had decided to do this, and had not thought of these as potential consequences, as they had enjoyed a few beers. The fact that they had taken the beers from the seized drink from a club that was a court exhibit, that they had drunk the beers on duty, that they had basically stolen and interfered with evidence, it was on their own heads.

Outside in the station office the early turn control staff filtered in. Usually, as one officer came in their night duty counterpart left. This morning they all stayed in, then as a group they all came out, subdued and heads down. They walked as a group to the stairs at the front of the building on their way to the superintendent's office, or the canteen, to await CIB2.

CIB2 were the investigators of police, police who looked at police wrong doings. Hated by all, but a necessity it seemed. They arrived, woken from their sleep, suited, and booted. They filed in the front door, past the station officer, who buzzed them in. One of them grunted a greeting, the others just stared and looked at the officers who made eye contact with them as they filed in. They did not need directions, they had been here before, they splintered into different locations and purposefully approached different parts of the station. One to the station office, another to the property office, one to the charge room and one went up the stairs, no doubt to the superintendent office. He would be the highest-ranking officer, and as it was potentially an inspector involved to be investigated then he would be of a higher rank than that to investigate him. Usually, it would be at least two ranks higher.

Kath stood waiting with the others in the charge room, and the CIB2 officer asked to be talked through the bottles and the bags. The skipper carefully selecting his words and supporting them with the paperwork described what he had found. The officer grunted, asked for the statements they had done, and told them to carry the bags to the property office along the corridor. They took the bags, carried them through to property office where the other CIB2 officer stood. The bags were booked in, sealed in the cage, a metal cage that formed a part of the inner workings of the property office, usually used for drugs, cash or high value property. As the officers filed out a bewildered civilian property officer came in. Bought to a standstill, he stood surveying his office and the interlopers. No doubt wondering too whether he had committed an error, he was as honest as the day was long but, as had already been seen tonight, that did not stop the collateral damage these officers had created.

The door closed on the property officer and the CIB2 officers. The night duty skipper, Kath, and the jailer headed for their own locker rooms, to change and go home. Leaving behind them the night duty control staff, as well as the other officers, sat in huddles in the canteen, under the watchful eye of the CIB2 staff. They passed the front door in a small huddle, Kath on the way to the section house, the jailer and the skipper to their cars parked in the public car park. Walking together away from the station they saw the chief superintendent's car turn into the road, behind the wheel a stern-faced senior officer who no doubt was furious. They parted as they reached the section house, hardly a word spoken between them. They would be back at work soon and no doubt there would be changes.

Chapter Eight

The last night of night duty. Kath woke from her troubled sleep. It was going to be a hard shift tonight, not only as tomorrow morning they left work at 6.30 am and would be back to a late shift at the latest at 2.30 pm, having at best seven hours sleep between shifts, but the fiasco of the night before would impact heavily on the team. She realised that even though they had no choice, there would be some officers who felt that they should not have counted the bottles, nor made statements of their findings. Likewise, it was possible some officers would not be on shift tonight either.

She stumbled through her ablutions, collecting together her uniform, and bulling her boots. She didn't feel hungry, yet she knew she would have to eat, or she would be struggling during the rest of the shift. She made her way to canteen in the section house. Usually, a place of hustle and bustle, this afternoon it was, thankfully, quiet, as she sat on her own in the canteen and waited for the food to be served, she thought back to the shift.

She'd had a good 'body' in, the evidence was good, she had actually had a very good week, and she would be in her skipper's good books for that. Yet the night shift officers drink up had left her feeling angry, frustrated, upset and many more emotions she couldn't find words to describe. They had taken away her own autonomy and had made her and others collateral damage, as they had not thought further than their drink. The repercussions could not be guessed at, at best discipline, at worst there was prosecution for some officers. While the collateral damage, such as the trust and integrity of others, would be questioned now, and in the future. The future, everything about this incident reminded her that there was a future, and these officers would provoke internal investigations, civil actions and cases being dropped. Anything that they had touched would be perceived to be tainted, not because it was, but the perceptions were there. The reputation of individuals, the station, the force was all shifting in an uncontrolled way, judgements would be made about honest and integrity now and for years to come.

Kath pulled herself together, there was nothing she could do to change the outcome, she was as boxed in as the others and she had to ride the storm, with the other collateral damage. She moved to the counter, took her food, and sat and ate. Her mind now fixed and determined that this was not going to ruin her day, week, or even her probation. Finished, finally, with her food, she collected the last things together and nervously walked to the station to commence the last shift of the week. She joined in the vein of blue that trickled in from car parks, section houses, tube stations and buses, all meeting at the station. Slowly making their way down to the basement, uniformed and ready to go.

The parade room was empty when she arrived. No smoke

haze, no noise. She sat staring ahead, one by one, officers quietly came in. Sitting, looking around, not meeting each other's eyes. The room filled, all the chairs were taken, but there was little noise.

The doors opened at the end of the parade room, and a new authoritative voice called through. 'Parade'. The room shot into action. Seated officers now stood, chairs forgotten behind them, all stood to attention, even the old sweats. A new skipper walked in, looking like a drill instructor from Hendon. Bulled immaculate boots that echoed as he stepped in, razor sharp creases in his jacket and trousers, flat cap with a sharp peak, that seemed to touch his nose. Looking every bit the soldier in a police uniform. Behind him stepped an equally immaculate inspector. Brisk authoritative movements almost marching into the room, in step with the sergeant, and looking every bit as formidable. Then behind the inspector was the chief superintendent and superintendent both in full uniform.

If the officer's backs could have achieved any further straightening at the sight of the two most senior officers in the station they did now. Officers stared into the fixed foreground.

The newcomers went to the chairs at the front of the room. The senior officers taking the two chairs while the parade ground staff stood behind them, in almost identical positions on either side. Looking like statutes, they held they formal positioning ridged and looking ahead.

Seconds passed; the senior officers did not ask the relief to sit down. No one would dare move until the order was given, if it ever was.

From the depths of the chief superintendent rumbled a voice that was as hard as the granite look on his face.

'These two officers are new to the team; they will be filling a vacancy that has arisen.'

He paused, the two officers now released from the spell, took the time to look from one officer on parade to the next. None dared to make eye to eye contact not even the old sweats.

The chief super continued.

'Last night there were several', he paused, 'irregularities, these are being looked at as we speak. There will be other officers filling any vacancy that might arise. Last night the behaviour of some officers has tainted the reputation of this station, the Met and us all. It will not be tolerated. CIB2 will speak to all of you during the next few days and I will expect you to fully co-operate. In the meantime, as we speak CIB are at present searching all your lockers.'

There was a sharp intake of breaths. Several faces suddenly lost their colour and took on a strange hue in the muted light of the parade room.

'If any additional things are found that require any further investigation you will be called back to the canteen. Otherwise from here you may all get a coffee, or start your patrols, as needed as soon as you have been posted.'

With that the two senior officers stood, walked out the hushed room. No one had said a word, no one had moved. The skipper half turned as if on a drill and walked to the door, he checked outside to see that the senior officers had gone. Then nodded to the inspector. They both swept off their hats and the skipper growled 'at ease, please be seated.' As both he and the inspector took the now vacated seats at the front of the room.

Still the only sounds were chairs scuffing as the parade room sat looking at the two new officers. The old sweats more comfortable now, staring at the interlopers, trying to exert their control over the newcomers. Instead of being met with shifting gazes the old sweats were met with firm stares that exuded confidence and knowledge of their position. Forcing the old sweats to look away, an unaccustomed experience for them, they were used to being the top dog.

The inspector started to speak. He did not shout, nor raise his voice, in the silence of the room he could be heard, as Kath looked out the corner of her eye, she noticed others like herself leaning forward as if pulled by an invisible string. The inspector's voice was strong, effortlessly determined and reeked of confidence.

'Today when we re parade, you will all look the part.'

He looked directly at the old sweats.

'Your uniforms will be ironed, shirts, jackets, trousers or skirts. Your hair will be cut to the regulation length, you will ensure that you have your shoes bulled or at the very least polished and brushed. You will parade with all your appointments and you will all be on time; you will not smoke in here or in uniform outside the police station. Any questions?'

There were obviously none, the request, no order, was simple, this is what you should be doing anyway, so you will do it, regardless of whether you have to get your hair cut on a quick change over.

The new section skipper took over, delivered the briefing as if he had been there all day memorising it, and posted officers to their respective beats. They were then dismissed. Some officers warily looking around, the same officers who had been shocked to hear the lockers were being spun. Still around the station were officers in suits moving from room to room, some carrying papers and some carrying exhibit bags.

The relief grabbed their radios, hurriedly grabbed a Styrofoam cup of coffee or tea from the canteen. The till was closed Kath noticed, the money went in and was cashed in. She had never seen that happen. Then the officers singularly went out on their beats or paired up to go to their vehicles for the night. Kath was posted again with the van driver, they drove out in the night, quietly contemplating the goings on. Not daring to speak to each other. The radio was silent, Sunday night, then as the time passed on the radio squawked messages from the control room from unfamiliar staff who were in there tonight, to first one then another officer to return to the station and report to the canteen. Thankfully the night passed and neither Simon nor Kath were called.

Although she was now Commissioner these early days had shaped the way she was. They would, combined with the experiences she had bought to the job, be the making of her. They had helped her to see the worth of a good team of people, but also that it was the team that had to be trusted and honest, and they were made up of individuals with their own baggage. It also made her realise that with the even greater power that she now had as the Commissioner she had greater responsibility to ensure that the past and the future were different commodities. That the past shaped the future, but the present was also important. She would, and had, and will, make sure that the Met was an organisation that officers past and present were proud of. She looked in the mirror one last time, smiled back at her reflection, and jauntily touched her hat in mock salute as she made her way to the meeting. Her reflections out of her mind now as she concentrated once more on the present and the future.

Disclaimer:

No one character is based on any one individual, though composite characters have been formed. Events are based on myth and composite incidents and may factually bear some resemblance to events in the past.